MIDNIGHT IN YOUR ARMS

MIDNIGHT IN YOUR ARMS

MORGAN KELLY

AVONIMPULSE
An Imprint of HarperCollinsPublishers

Excerpt from *The Forbidden Lady* copyright © 2002, 2012 Kerrelyn Sparks.

Excerpt from *Turn to Darkness* copyright © 2012 Tina Wainscott.

EPub Edition NOVEMBER 2012 ISBN: 9780062242600

Print Edition ISBN: 9780062242617

10 9 8 7 6 5 4 3 2 1

For Neil, the hero of my real-life love story

CHAPTER ONE

London
October 1926

Laura Dearborn dreamed about Stonecross Hall long before she ever saw it.

It had haunted her dreams ever since she was a child and her uncanny gifts began to strengthen. The house she dreamed of so often was more than just a house—it was like a person, with a character and personality so strong and overwhelming, Laura often felt as though it was *watching* her, even during her waking hours. After she had learned more about her psychic gifts and the power of the subconscious mind, she believed that the house of which she dreamed—looming, foreboding, and in many ways terribly, achingly sad—was some sort of dark personification of herself, her own deep and shadowed places. She had no idea then that the place was all too real, and that she *belonged* to it, and it to her.

Though she had been born with her powers, it wasn't until after the Great War that Laura finally allowed herself to use them. Before then, she had always been afraid. Afraid of everything, really. But then the world had gone mad, and Laura, like most people, lost everything, and nothing much seemed worth being afraid over anymore. The horrors she had witnessed in the medical tents on the Western Front were so much worse than anything she could encounter through the palm of some poor soul's hand, or in the tea leaves swirling at the bottom of a china cup. Her powers were all Laura had left of her former life. When she came back to England, she put her uniform away, bobbed her hair, took a flat in Piccadilly, and set up shop with her deck of tarot cards and spirit board at her kitchen table. Women flocked to her in droves. Before she knew what had happened, she had a reputation all over London as a girl who knew what she was about—a girl with a gift.

It had all begun with the other nurses, of course, girls who had lost their sweethearts, cousins, brothers, and friends in the trenches. After the war, they started coming to her, for some reassurance, a way of forging a link forever severed, a chance to move on and make new lives for themselves with the men England still had left to offer. Laura found she had quite a knack for communing with the dead. Even after the cards had been put away and the planchette stilled, she felt the way the dead clamored around her, clinging to her, trying to come through. The dead, like the living, were desperate to make a connection, to hold on to what remained of them on the earthly plane. They were so thick in the air around her that Laura sometimes felt as though she was breathing not air but ghosts.

Laura did her best to comfort them, to send them on their way to whatever rest awaited them. She wasn't sure if she believed in an afterlife, though the men who had died so horribly on both sides of the war had certainly earned a sweet release. She was certain that clinging to a life that had been ripped from them was not in any way a good thing. She didn't want the dead to stay, though they were her bread and butter. And she was the last person who should be counseling other souls about moving on. She certainly had not done so. She lived in a limbo of her own, had made it far too comfortable. She was afraid that there was nothing else out there for her, that her life had already been lived, the barrel well and truly scraped clean. Truth be told, though she claimed to aid the living, it was the dead she wanted to help. After all, she had more in common with them, for all that her heart still beat and ached and fluttered, as any living heart should.

It was a lonely life. Laura had never had many friends, except for the other nurses she had served with on the Front. None of her particular friends lived anywhere near her, and many of them had their own concerns, the remnants of their families to hold together as best they could as they struggled to make a life for themselves in the aftermath. England was not the same. The whole world had changed, and not for the better, despite the victory they had won at such great cost. Perhaps that was the problem. The cost had been far too great for the survivors to feel much like rejoicing. At best, they managed a cautious contentment. At worst, their lives were an utter ruin. Laura's generation drank and danced and took strangers to bed, struggling to find a place in the world, a context for their lives—but they were lost, like children left behind in the woods to forage for themselves, alone. It was like some terrible cautionary tale in which the moral made no sense.

Laura had been luckier than most. She had lost her brother, Charles, who, though he was her whole family, was only one person. Some women lost every man they had ever known. Although heartbroken by the loss of her brother, Laura had no sweetheart or husband to lose, and likely never would have, now that the male populace of England had been so greatly depleted. Those left were the walking wounded, never to be the same strapping, joyful boys again, sauntering about the boroughs of London as if the entire city was their own. It was as though London had become half-peopled with ghosts. Which was a good business for people like Laura, and for those who pretended to be like her—the charlatans and the opportunists who rapped tables and rattled spoons and swallowed gauze they later retched up, claiming it to be the ectoplasmic residue of the beloved dead.

Laura didn't go in for such parlor tricks, which disappointed some of her potential clients, who wanted the full theatrical show for their shillings. Instead, she told them the truth, firmly and clearly, with no hysterics. Those who looked for the comfort of reality came to her, and came again, and told everyone they knew. Laura was busy from sunup to sundown, when she finally locked her door, turned her lamps down low, and ate her small supper alone with the cat, who never asked her for a thing, cats being unconcerned with the state of their dead. Felines were very practical that way, which was why Laura liked them. She knew her cat would have done very well without her and needed nothing she could give him, not even the saucer of milk set on the windowsill. He stayed with her because he wanted to, and consequently, he was the nicest thing in her life.

Laura went to bed tired every night, and a few pounds richer than she had been when she woke up—all of her uneasy lucre locked up in an old money box that had belonged to her grandfather, who had once been a greengrocer. She took money for what she did because it was the sort of transaction that needed to be balanced. People did not like her for what she did for them. They felt beholden to her. Paying her a set fee assuaged the feeling that they owed her for something more than could be bought. Even so, Laura's clients never felt fully caught up on their bill. They scurried away as fast as they could, after she had told them what she could and communicated what was possible to the dead. Laura often went to bed sick at heart because the only people she could really talk to were on the other side of the dark river all must cross in their time.

Despite this, Laura had invitations from people she didn't know well, to parties thrown by the bohemian social elite, many of whom were her new clients. They threw lavish soirees in the jazz clubs of Piccadilly, some of which lasted for days. The tabloid papers called them the Bright Young Things, but it was a terrible irony. There was nothing bright nor particularly youthful in their haggard, glazed expressions, addled with drink and opium. Still, sometimes Laura longed to join them, and on a rare occasion, she slipped down the stairs in a cheap synthetic-silk frock to dance and drink among them in the club below, fierce as any of the lost girls and boys who had found their way back out of the forest only to find their country half-deserted. Dancing didn't make her happy. She didn't think it made any of them happy. It was more like a ritual bloodletting, a catharsis no one else needed or understood. Sometimes, Laura danced alone in her flat, the music thrumming up through the floorboards, vibrating through her whole body until she was slick with sweat and her heart beat against the cage of her ribs, frenetic and wild, as though impaling itself on the music, on her body's need to escape her mind.

And then, inevitably, almost nightly, she dreamed of the house that had haunted her all of her remembered life.

It was a large house—massive, even. The sort of house the very rich had built for themselves as country retreats in the past century: decadent, sprawling, monumental. Like a tomb, a mausoleum ready-made for the future generations of the rich. Many such houses had been turned into convalescent homes for the wounded during the war, and some of them had stayed that way for a time after. Laura herself had worked in one of them in Kent for a while, before being discharged and returning to London. She had never much liked the house she had worked in. It was stuffy and smug, far too ostentatious. She always felt as though all the portraits of the great family's ancestors were watching every movement, every single thing she did as she moved through the illustrious rooms with her basins of blood, vomit, and night soil, and as though they were wrinkling up their noses. *They died for you!* she wanted to shout. *For your children! For your bloody England that will never thank them, could never thank them enough, for what they have done, all they have sacrificed.* But it was no more good shouting at the portraits than it ever was shouting at the dead, or those who tried so desperately to cling to them.

The house she dreamed of was not like the house in which she had worked. While her dream house was little more than an abandoned shell, the house in which she had been a nurse was still living, still had life in it. There was a sense that its life was, in a way, greater than any that had been lived in its walls, that its vitality would go on and on forever. The house in her dreams was very much dead. It was the skeleton of a house, with the wind blowing through it, scattered with the dead leaves of many decades past. It clung to rocky cliffs above a vast and tumultuous sea that licked up at it, as if to pull it down. It was the ghost of a house only, and Laura knew what to do with ghosts. At least, she *usually* did. But this house wasn't real. There was no exorcising it with a gentle incantation, a few candles, and an exhortation to move on. This house was a part of her, a part of her own mind. To be rid of it was to be rid of some part of herself she didn't really recognize or understand.

Or so she thought, until the day the solicitor showed up, briefcase in hand, to knock diffidently at her door.

It hadn't been a particularly good day. Laura was tired. She had a headache. Her normally inquisitive brown eyes had become hazy with the sort of pain that results from too many spirits trying to climb right into her, as though she was some sort of sanctuary. Laura did *not*, as some mediums did, allow the dead to use her body. Fighting them off was a difficult and wearying battle, and some spirits were stronger and more insistent than others. The day of the solicitor's visit was a very trying one indeed, and she almost cried when she heard the polite but insistent knock on the door just as the kettle was coming to a boil and her bit of soup had started to warm on the stove.

"I'm taking no more clients for the day," she called through the door, not even bothering to open it. She was so tired she was literally drooping, her blouse untucked and her hair in wild disarray. She wanted no one to see her in such a state. She patted at her hair absently, as though the visitor could somehow see her right through the door. If she wasn't so tired herself, she could certainly have seen him or her—it was part of her gift, and helped her to feel much more secure about opening the door to perfect strangers, day in and day out. But her mind was clouded, and the door blocked the person from her mind's eye, as though Laura was any other person with an unwelcome visitor.

The person knocked again, and she sighed in exasperation, closing her eyes. "Please, go away! Come back tomorrow morning, after nine o'clock, and I'll see you then."

"Miss Dearborn, I am not a client of yours," a pleasant, even rather genial voice said clearly and distinctly through the door. "Rather, you are something of a client of mine, and I really think you'd better hear what I have to say. You don't have to say a word, only listen, though I suspect you will have more than a few questions for me."

Laura stared at the door, considering. She could insist that the fellow come back the next day; after all, it could be a ruse, a manipulation that would force her to see a client so desperate he could actually force himself to sound quite reasonable. She had met people like that many times before, and at the moment, she had no defense whatsoever against such machinations other than the strong oak door and deadbolt that now stood between her and the man on the other side.

And yet, here was her hand, reaching out.

Before she knew what she was doing, Laura found herself

unlocking the door. She squared her shoulders as she opened it a minimal amount, just enough to get a good look at her visitor. She arranged her face into as bland an expression as possible before looking her trespasser in the face.

"Yes?" she said coolly.

The stranger's expression was equally nondescript, but remained attentive, polite, and entirely benign. He was well dressed, his hair brushed smoothly back from his brow. He had the sort of face belonging to so many well-to-do, middle-class Englishmen that they seemed not so much a demographic of people but a family with so many members that they seemed to populate half of London entirely on their own. He was young enough to have seen some action during the war, but seemed so entirely unscathed that Laura took an instant and uncharitable dislike to him, simply for having made the choice to escape what so many others not only *could* not, but *would* not. When she looked at him, she saw yet another living, breathing, unjustly spared stand-in for her brother, who had drowned in his own blood at Passchendaele.

The man smiled, and there was more of a personality to him than Laura had originally imagined. His face crinkled pleasantly, like the face of someone's kindly bachelor brother, and Laura relaxed slightly. She knew she had been unkind. She had no right imagining she knew the truth about the living simply because she so clearly understood the dead. Her face softened, and she opened the door a few inches wider, so that her full face and body could be seen.

"What may I do for you, Mr. . . . ?"

"Tisdale. James Lawrence Tisdale. And it isn't what you

may do for me, Miss Dearborn, but what I am about to do for you."

"I am not interested in a new carpet sweeper just at present, Mr. Tisdale," Laura said tolerantly. "One of your colleagues was here just the other day, and as I told him, I'm quite satisfied with the carpet sweeper I've got. So if you will please excuse me, my supper is about to boil over."

"I assure you, dear lady, I am no salesman." Mr. Tisdale chuckled again good-naturedly, despite the slight, and this time Laura could see the prosperous glint of a gold crown in his easy smile.

She narrowed her eyes, understanding dawning at last. "You're a lawyer, aren't you?"

The man raised his hands in mock surrender. "Guilty as charged, Miss. I come from Beckett, Tisdale, and Roe, and we are solicitors—have been for several generations, in point of fact. Which is, in a way, all part of why I stand before you today. With your permission, Miss Dearborn, I would like to step inside and discuss a rather significant and delicate matter with you in the privacy of your flat. This is not at all a frivolous call, I assure you."

Laura looked at him for a moment longer, and he gazed back at her gravely, waiting for her to decide. She had a feeling he would wait for as long as he must, that she could stand here considering him for an hour, and he would let her. It was this sort of endearing, canine quality that finally decided her. After all, she allowed total strangers into her home all day long between the hours of nine and six o'clock, with a hypothetical break for tea that she rarely took. She spent most of the day tired and ravenous, bombarded by the emotionally needy. What was another hour without her supper, and another stranger at her table? This one at least said he wanted nothing from her, that he wanted to give her something. Or at least, *do* something for her. Which was enough of a rarity in her life that she was intrigued.

She sighed, and opened the door fully, gesturing for him to come in. He did so diffidently, though his eyes darted around her dismal little flat with great interest. She flushed when his gaze lingered on the portrait of Charles in his uniform, which was the sole decoration on her mantel.

"Sweetheart?" he inquired.

"Brother," Laura replied flatly.

He nodded with true sympathy. "I lost a brother myself. His name was William, but we called him Bill. It was a terrible shock to my poor mother. He was to have come into the firm as well, you see, but . . ." He shrugged.

Laura stared at him. He went a little pink, as if embarrassed to have told her so much. "It's quite alright, Mr. Tisdale," she said, with a deprecating smile. "I have that effect on people. If you will please follow me."

He did so meekly enough, taking the chair she offered him at the scuffed kitchen table where she did her readings and channelling. She set a cup and saucer down in front of him, and another for herself. "Tea?"

"Please."

"Cream? I've no lemon, I'm afraid."

"Black will do just fine, Miss Dearborn."

She nodded, and measured the tea leaves into the pot before adding the water. She set it down on the trivet to steep before finally taking her place across from the preternaturally patient solicitor.

"I suppose you're wondering what all the mystery is about, Miss Dearborn."

Laura shrugged, though she was growing rather curious, and not a little apprehensive. She couldn't read Mr. Tisdale. The living were not at all her speciality, but she had learned a few things during her years nursing the nearly dead and irretrievably wounded—not to mention those who survived them. But Mr. Tisdale was kindly, jovial, and completely locked away inside of himself. He was not a man who displayed his secrets as most people did, although Laura had a feeling he had more than a few. But his secrets were none of her concern. She looked at the surface of him, and decided to deal only with what she could see: a man with something important to tell her. Something that may change her life, whether she wanted it to or not.

"Go on," she said.

"Miss Dearborn, I am here on behalf of Stonecross Hall."

Laura Dearborn, consummate stalwart, felt punched in the gut. Her heart started to pound painfully in her chest, and her lungs felt as though they could take only the shallowest of breaths. Her fingertips began to tingle as they did only when she was about to encounter the most powerful of channellings. Her ears rang, flooded with the noise of a hundred wireless stations gone off air. *Stonecross Hall. So that's what it's called.*

She took hold of herself, firmly and calmly. "I have never heard of it," she said. She picked up the teapot to pour, and to her great relief, her hands were completely steady.

"Well, I am here to tell you that it has most certainly heard of you."

Laura emitted a short laugh. "That is utterly preposterous. How can a house hear of anyone?"

He chuckled. "Fair enough. What I meant to say was that the house has very much to do with you. You see, Miss Dearborn, Stonecross Hall is yours."

Laura's mind raced, her thoughts forming unbidden. *Of course it is. It always has been mine, and I its . . .* She struggled to repress the rush of thoughts, her visage unmoved, her brow maintaining the shape of polite skepticism.

"How is that possible?" she said evenly, taking a sip, and not even flinching as the boiling liquid scalded her tongue. She couldn't feel a thing. She was utterly numb—whether with anticipation or with dread, she couldn't tell. She was an automaton, a doll, dancing on invisible strings. *Strings that tie me to Stonecross,* she thought, absently. The whole thing was ridiculous.

"This is absurd," she said. "I've never owned anything in my life. I have no family, no connections. Just how is it that I've come to own a house?"

"It was left to you by the last person ever to own the house, by the family name of Storm."

"And are they distant relations of mine? I've never heard of them until now."

"No, Miss Dearborn. In fact, no living member of the family has existed in quite some time."

"I don't understand. Then who has made me the beneficiary of the house?"

"A Mr. Alaric Storm the Third."

A ridiculous name, like something straight out of a penny novel. "I was not aware of having been known to a Mr. Alaric Storm, of any numeral."

"You aren't. In fact, you could not possibly be known to Mr. Storm, Miss Dearborn, as the gentleman in question died thirty-five years ago."

"I am only twenty-eight."

"Just so."

"Therefore, Mr.—Storm, was it?—died nearly ten years before I was born!"

"Precisely."

"I . . . I am at a loss. This makes no sense whatsoever."

"Indeed it does not. And yet, here we are."

"If Mr. Storm died thirty-five years ago and left his house to me in his will, why is it I am only hearing of it now?"

"You mean, why were you not made aware of the bequest for so many years?"

"Indeed. I should have been very glad of a house at many times in my life. How is it that I am being given one at precisely the time when I need it least?"

Mr. Tisdale didn't make any reference to the shabby state of their surroundings. He did not even seem to be thinking of it, and Laura was absurdly grateful to him. "The will stipulated that the house should not be bequeathed until the occasion of your twenty-eighth birthday. Which, I am sure you will recall, is in fact today. So here I am."

Laura was more than a little astounded. Was it really her birthday? Was she really only just twenty-eight? Twenty-eight might not be particularly young, but on her best days, she felt forty-five when her sessions were finished and she turned in for the night. If she was lucky, she would rise feeling only marginally younger—a sprightly *thirty*-eight, most days. At any rate, she hadn't celebrated her birthday since before the war, when she had been an impossibly naïve young girl.

Mr. Tisdale patted her hand kindly, bringing her back to herself. "Happy Birthday, Miss Dearborn," he said with a grin. "You, my dear woman, are an heiress of no inconsiderable fortune and property. I must say, this has been a curious undertaking. It isn't often one must wait for one's client to be born before bestowing upon her a bequest."

Laura nodded absently, only half listening as he prattled on. It was a dream. It had to be a dream. She looked at the papers Mr. Tisdale laid before her without seeing them. She took up the pen he offered her without feeling the weight of it in her hand, and signed the places he indicated without consciously remembering her own name. In a trice, it was done. She was a rich woman. She owned a house in the country. She need never work for pay again, and more importantly, she need never speak to another ghost for as long as she lived.

CHAPTER TWO

Stonecross Hall
October 1866

A decade had passed since the war ended, yet Alaric still dreamed of the Crimea. It was his constant ghost, that distant, nebulous peninsula where so many of his friends had died, mostly of disease, more than a few of gunshot or bayonet wounds. Alaric himself had earned a lamed leg to accompany the experience, and for what profit? None that he had ever been able to discern. He had left part of himself behind on the shores of the Baltic Sea, and part of that dark and unfathomable water had come back with him, replacing some part of him that had once been essential. No one remarked much on the change, not after so many years. But they knew he was not the same man and never would be.

Alaric sat before the fire in his bedchamber, allowing its warmth to dry his freshly bathed skin and hair as he sipped moodily at his pre-dinner *aperitif*. It was in moments like these, the silent torture of reflection before he took part in yet another meaningless daily ritual, that his memories of war were strongest. He remembered what it was like to eat then, the ravenous hunger that overtook him when he was a soldier and his meals were scanty. Why had they seemed like such banquets? What was it about rations shared with comrades who would not see the light of dawn that made the food taste so much like ambrosia, while the meals he shared with those nearest and dearest to him often took on the flavor of ashes? Perhaps it was as simple as the fact that none of them had ever truly been hungry. They ate for pleasure, and yet would never know the brutal sensuality of eating a meal likely to be their last.

Alaric poured another glass. He drank whiskey greedily enough. He better endured the company of civilians when he had a few drams in him.

They thought they understood war, his friends and relations who had stayed at home, eagerly devouring every word in the press, goggling at all of the photographs plastered across the pages of *The Times*. No war had ever been so accurately documented in every gruesome particular. No citizenry had ever been so close to a war while remaining comfortably at home, playing the pianoforte in their parlors, smoking and sipping brandy in their drawing rooms after partaking of plentiful dinners, and laughing raucously over billiards while Alaric and his friends were shot to pieces for no reason whatsoever. Parts of them froze and fell off into the bleakness of the Russian winter while less patriotic (and perhaps less idiotic) Englishmen nodded off during church, exasperating their wives into fresh throes of domestic despair. Alaric had never been so cold in his life as he was when he was eighteen, practically a boy soldier. He had never been fully warm since, no matter how the fires of Stonecross Hall

blazed and the chandeliers glittered. They were nothing but
marsh-lights toward which he wandered, without ever finding their warmth. They taunted him, and still he stumbled
after them in the dark.

His dreams were not all gruesome. Many of them were
beautiful, full of a peculiar purple light: dawn breaking over
the drifted snow, the sun pulling threads of light from the
trees and weaving from them fairy stories. In his dreams, he
walked between the snow-blanketed bodies of the dead and
felt a peace he did not feel in his waking hours. When he
dreamed, for one thing, he did not limp. He was as whole as
he had been as a child, and just as quick. It was true that the
limp was far less pronounced than it had been when he first
came home, an invalid, full of fever and rage. He could even
dance a quadrille now, if he so chose—but he rarely did. He
had quite lost his taste for it now that he spent his life dancing around and between the outstretched arms of the dead,
begging for a partner to drag them from their listlessness. He
was afraid of how willing he was to oblige them.

He knew it was past time he recovered and moved on with
his life. It was more than time that he should be married, a
father to the children who would inherit Stonecross after he
had gone to his rest. The problem was that he didn't much
like the idea of saddling a defenseless child with the consider-
able tonnage of his ancestral home. It did not sit easy on his
shoulders, and never had, even before the war. Now, it was
well-nigh intolerable. It was worse than a ghost, this house of
his. Inside of it, Alaric had the uncanny feeling that *he himself*
was the ghost, that he was haunting his house, and it was just
biding its time until his life should be done. The house no

longer liked him—it only tolerated him. Stonecross knew he was not the same. His dearest wish was to get away, for good. The only time he had ever managed to do so, other than his time away at school—which was only ever temporary—he had come back maimed for his trouble. He had stayed home ever since. He didn't have much left to lose, and he wanted to keep to himself what little remained.

Alaric rose, and fumbled with his glass, shoving it back in place next to the cut crystal decanter that always seemed to sparkle so alluringly on his mantel. He had long left off the pretense of keeping liquor solely in the drawing room for guests and after-dinner relaxation. Everyone knew the master of Stonecross liked his liquor.

He crossed the room, and stood at the window he liked to keep thrown open, though he knew the housemaids clucked and said he would catch his death. Girls like that, plain and good-hearted, would never understand how a man like him could half want something like that, half hope for the kind of death a cold breeze could bring in from the sea that glimmered in the night like an eye that saw all, and cared little. Sometimes he wished he had been born into a simpler life, like the people who took care of his every comfort.

Of course, it was a foolish fancy. He knew nothing of the lives of others. He was rich. He was privileged. He was handsome and well respected, though it was a wary sort of respect. People did not feel about him the way they had when he was a boy, golden and gleaming, but they, too, managed to tolerate him admirably. Any unmarried daughter of *bon ton* would be more than happy to take him if he asked.

But if he was a ghost, the girls he knew were waifs. They

had no substance. No experience. No sense of the great wonder and pain of what it was to be a human animal. They weren't animals at all; that was by and large the problem with the pampered and ornamented lot of them. None of them had *suffered*. Alaric had grown to respect the results of suffering on the human soul, if one could suffer sensibly, learn from it, and gain a little wisdom. He wasn't sure he had managed to do so, but he had an idea that if he was acquainted with a woman who had also suffered, they might, together, learn what to make of it. The girls with whom he was daily surrounded, herded by their ambitious mamas and indulgent papas, draped in jewels, silks, and suitors, were like so many automatons. They were clever marionettes, equipped with all the elegant gestures of well-bred womanhood, the correct demeanors bred into their very bones, but they had no true life-spark of their own. They were only wind-up girls.

He lived with a woman of that sort, if someone who was still so much a girl could properly be called a woman. Ellen Wright was a distant cousin and his family's ward. They had been famous friends in childhood, and before he went away to war, he had made a fervent declaration to the little chit that he had almost immediately regretted. Even then, she had changed, morphed from a jolly playmate into an ambitious young debutante. To her credit, she had never married anyone else, and Ellen had a fortune of her own. She could have married a dozen times over, but she hadn't. Instead, she had remained installed in Stonecross, taking her place as the woman of the house after Alaric's mother died, as though it was quite within her rights. And perhaps it was. He had said as much, once, when he was young and foolish, and hadn't known yet what life really meant. Then, it was all a splendid parlor game, and he a prince at play. Ellen had always thought to be his princess.

That was quite impossible now, of course, but she had never quite understood that particular message. Perhaps she thought to wear him down. And maybe he should just let her. There were worse things than a pretty, vapid wife who would see to all the entertainments and make sure all the appropriate seasonal sentiments were expressed. She would make certain they went to Town in the correct week, and returned to the country when it was most fashionable to do so. Except that Alaric had no mind ever to go to London again. He was finished with balls and dinner parties, with forays to the opera and the pleasure gardens. He didn't care to visit the club, or have himself fitted by an exclusive tailor for suits of clothes he would discard after the Season ended. He hadn't even been bothering to have his hair cut lately—it hung long and thick to his shoulders. It was enough that he remembered to have himself shaved and dressed in a fresh shirt and clean cravat in time for dinner. He better remembered to refill his glass while he moped by the fire, and turn the pages as he read his book. He would be happy to malinger at Stonecross forever if everyone would just leave him in bloody peace.

They wouldn't, of course. It was about to be his birthday. He would be thirty. There was to be a party. He didn't *want* a bloody party, but what *he* wanted had very little to do with it. Ellen had her heart set on a party, and an engagement announcement, no doubt. Alaric wondered if he would oblige her. He hadn't made up his mind yet. Everything would be simpler if he did, in many ways. After all, he couldn't go on living at Stonecross with him with only his father to chaperone, an ailing man who paid little attention to what was happening around him. It simply wasn't done.

Alaric turned from the window, impatient with the view, which never changed. It was always the same black liquid shimmering in moonlight, with the clouds moving too fast over the sky for him to find any recognizable shape. He was impatient, too, thinking about Ellen. She was not the sort of person who took up much space in a well-stocked mind. She was pretty, and intelligible enough. But Alaric's mind slipped so easily away from her. She would do much better to marry someone else, someone for whom beauty and wealth were more alluring.

Alaric kept hoping that if he bored her to death on a daily basis, Ellen would decide to leave, and make her own way with the fortune she had come into on her twenty-first birthday. That had been a damnably long time ago. What was she now—twenty-eight or nine? She was getting dangerously close to being left on the shelf. Only her beauty and her fortune stopped people's tongues wagging—much. An unmarried woman her age with a perfectly eligible bachelor in her daily midst would always set people talking. No doubt people thought them secret lovers, and that he refused to marry her and she had nowhere else to turn, or some scandalous rubbish of that sort. Such things did go on, he knew. Which was why he should perhaps just marry her and have done with it. A gentleman would have done so years ago. She had certainly earned it, living with him as he was for so long, putting her best face on while the ladies of the *ton* whispered behind their fans.

Another reason he ought to marry her was that perhaps she actually loved him. Stranger things did happen. She made all the pretty little gestures and unspoken declarations that maidens in love affected. Could it be real?

He didn't think so.

There was a coolness to Ellen, something he thought of as innocence and virtue when they were children. He thought she would warm up when womanhood came upon her, but she never did. There was something calculating about her. She was slightly . . . serpentine. That was the bare truth of it, and he was repelled by her manner, which was unnatural. He didn't love her. He couldn't. And he still harbored a childish fancy that he would like to marry a woman he loved.

Certainly he didn't *need* to marry. No gentleman did, except for the getting of progeny, which concerned him not at all. His nephew Freddy would inherit Stonecross, though the child had more than enough estate and fortune of his own. Alaric's sister, Lizzie, had married very well indeed. They would be coming to Stonecross for the party, of course, even though he had written Lizzie not to. *Why not, darling?* she had written back gaily. *I've nothing better to do, after all. London is frightfully dull this time of year.* Alaric was of the opinion that the sooty city was frightfully dull at *every* time of year, but he hadn't bothered arguing. Like Ellen, Lizzie would do as she liked.

Alaric sighed as the bell gonged to signal the family to dress for dinner, though it would be a dismal affair, with only himself and Ellen. His father didn't eat in company any longer, but took his meals on a tray in his bedchamber. Alaric wished he could get away with doing the same. He didn't feel like eating but he would not do Ellen the discourtesy of failing to appear. He was still something of a gentleman, if only a paltry one, and she had done nothing to deserve rudeness. It wasn't her fault that she had become so tiresome. No doubt he had, too. Staying too long buried away at Stonecross would transform even the most sparkling personality into that of a complete dullard. No wonder Ellen wanted a party. He would let her have it and be as gracious about it as he could.

Jeffries, his valet, came silently into the room with the shaving set he kept in perfect order. Alaric allowed him to scrape away the prickling stubble, evidence of one more day spent in aristocratic indolence. He was shaved daily because Ellen liked to see him clean and smooth. Alaric wouldn't bother if it wasn't for her scrutinizing gaze, any more than he would bother putting on the dark blue dressing gown she had given him for Christmas. He knew how much it would hurt her feelings if he didn't wear it, even though she never saw him in it.

He sat down before the glass to allow Jeffries to brush his damp hair, ignoring the man's disapproving throat noise as he handled its unfashionable length. Alaric gazed at himself by the light of the lamp that had been turned high on the dressing table, noticing how little shadow it managed to dispel. October really was the gloomiest month. He wondered why he had had the perversity to have been born in it. He much preferred May. Had he been born in May, no doubt he would have had a much more delightful personality.

When he was a child, his nanny had told him the most appalling stories about children who were born on All Hallows, as he had been. "They ain't like other children at all,

Master Alaric," she liked to tell him, with an ominous tone in her voice. Certainly, he didn't *feel* like an ordinary person with ordinary cares, and he always felt strangely restless in October, his skin creeping and crawling beneath his clothes. The world seemed suddenly uncanny, and watchful. He felt as though he was walking between worlds, which was how one was meant to feel, if one put any stock at all in the folk superstitions of people like Nanny, who was the granddaughter of a Devon hedge witch, if she was to be believed. As a child, Alaric had always believed her. In October, he believed her even now.

He tolerated being dressed with his customary indifference, allowing Jeffries to move him about like a child deploying a toy soldier. When he was perfectly presentable according to Jeffries's impeccable eye, the valet stood back and allowed Alaric to survey himself in the mirror. He did so as though it meant something to him, his face and his physique, the perfectly starched collar and beautifully tailored tailcoat that enclosed his body. He took in his reflection, noting that his jawline and hair were equally smooth, his clothing elegant and perfectly brushed. He looked as he always looked in the evenings, and that was all he asked. He nodded. "That will do, Jeffries. Thank you."

Alaric followed him out a moment later, turning left where Jeffries turned right. He descended the staircase just as the bell gonged a second time, signaling the imminence of his dinner. He tried to imagine hunger, but he hadn't been hungry in years. He had only been fed. He felt like a pet, a lapdog, listless and without use. He had once killed for his keep, and as little as he liked it, he had at least felt entitled to his dinner in the Crimea. That was something every man should feel at the close of the day.

That night, he ate even less at dinner than usual. Ellen chattered away animatedly, and he heard not a word she said. He didn't even bother making polite noises in his throat or wearing the expression of bemused inquiry that usually did the trick. He could see the irritated, troubled look come over her face again and again, the one she saved for when he was not behaving the way she wished. She wore that expression a lot lately.

"Alaric, have you heard a word I've said this whole blessed evening?" she demanded, after the third one of her amusing anecdotes fell flat.

"No," he said, before he could stop himself.

She stared at him, her expression souring slightly. "I see. I'm terribly sorry to be such a bore."

He sighed. "It's not your fault. You can't help it."

She gasped as though he had slapped her. "Really, Alaric!" was all she could manage. She never responded in kind when he snapped and bit at her heels. It *was* rather dull of her. He was spoiling for a good fight, even if it bore a veneer of politesse.

"I am a frightful bore, too," he said wryly, pushing her a little further. "It's this bloody house. It sucks all the luster out of life this time of year."

"Well, why don't we go away?" Ellen said, brightening, taking the opportunity he had opened for her to argue for yet another of her manias: travelling to fashionable resorts and watering holes, as if they didn't get quite enough of the sea where they sat, with it moaning through the very walls and windows that contained them. "We could go to Bath, or Brighton. The winters here are far too dull, you are right."

Alaric shook his head. "Why don't *you* go to Bath or Brighton, Ellen?" he said quietly. "Why didn't you go, years ago? You aren't growing any younger. Neither of us are."

Ellen lowered her head, tears standing out in her clear green eyes. "That is very unkind of you, Alaric, after all I've done for you."

"Ellen, I don't want to you to *do anything* for me. Can't you see that? I just want to be left in peace."

"I thought I could bring you peace," she said in a small voice. "I thought I could brighten your life. That is why I am throwing this party, you know. For you. I thought being surrounded by your friends might make you happy."

Alaric sighed and smiled warily, chagrined by her words. "I know," he said softly, as the gentleman that still resided somewhere inside of him rose again to the surface and took control. "Thank you, Ellen. It's very kind of you."

She reanimated immediately, taking what he said as a far more meaningful encouragement than was his intent. She chattered on through dessert, buoyed by his words, and he pretended to listen with more interest than he really felt. *Bloody hell*, he thought, with gathering apprehension as he looked at her glowing face. *If I am not careful, I really am going to have to marry the girl.*

"**W**hy not simply marry the girl?" His father's voice was hoarse, ragged with pain and the weariness of a death too long postponed. Alaric frowned, looking down at the face he no longer knew, spotted with age and worn away until it was little more than skin stretched over a bone frame. "After all, she cannot live here with you after I am gone, Alaric. You strain the boundaries of propriety as it is."

Alaric sighed, slumping down in his chair. He massaged his temples. Damn, but he had a headache. "I don't love her, Father. And I don't think she loves me. She loves . . . I don't know what she loves. But it isn't me. At best, it is some idea of me, a fantasy that will never come true. I think she believes somehow that if we were only married, the man she actually wants will appear out of the ether and take my place. Sometimes I feel as though when she looks at me, she sees that man's ghost."

He thought his father would dismiss his moribund notions with a frail wave of his hand, but to his surprise, the old man stared at him with a penetrating gaze. "If Ellen was capable of so complex a thought—and I am not convinced that she is—she would be right, would she not? As I am myself so close to becoming one, I think I am becoming rather adept at recognizing a ghost when I see one. My son, you're no more alive than your dear mother, God rest her."

Alaric stared. He might be sick unto death, but the old fellow was as astute as ever. To be so easily read touched a nerve, and Alaric spoke before he thought. "I do not know what you're talking of, Father," he said evenly, his tone light but humorless. "Perhaps the laudanum Doctor Wakefield prescribed is a little stronger than it should be."

"Don't condescend to me, boy. I am still your father, even if I am nearly dead." The old mad coughed, reddening, though whether from the effort of scolding his son or from emotion, it was difficult to say.

Alaric's heart gave a painful tug, contrition taking a firm grip on him. He leaned forward to take the old man's hand awkwardly in his own. They weren't much given to demonstration. "Forgive me, sir—I didn't mean what I said."

Alaric Storm the elder, second of his name, maintained his piercing gaze. He looked into his son's eyes, and the younger man flinched, pulling away to stand at the window. No one looked at him like that anymore—as if they could see straight into his core. He wasn't sure what resided in that ransacked place where, so he had been taught, his soul resided. He didn't think much on his soul anymore. He told himself he didn't believe in it, that when he was finished with his body, everything he was would go out like a snuffed candle. He didn't know whether the notion terrified or relieved him. This time of year, the spirit world seemed oddly close, as if he could reach out and touch it—or it him. He shouldn't make light of such things, or so Nanny had always told him, the old terror.

"We should never have let you go," his father murmured from the bed. "If we had known what it would do to you, we would have tied you to the bedstead until you saw reason."

Alaric stared out at the sea. The mullioned windows were salt-stained, and he felt as though he looked through a bleary eye that could perceive little more than the shifting of light over the bay. "If I wasn't so damnably weak, I would have forgotten, and gone on with my life by now," he replied. "It must shame you to have a son who cannot bear to live with things of which other men are deeply proud."

"Few men are made for war, Alaric. Those who are made for it are something more or perhaps less than human. Do not desire to be like them."

Alaric grimaced. "Father, please. Don't patronize me."

"It isn't patronage, it's good common sense."

Alaric shrugged noncommittally. He really didn't want to talk about it any longer. He began sketching a childish tracing on the glass. After a moment, he rubbed it out, and through the scrubbed glass he glanced down into the courtyard, in which the huge and ancient stone cross that lent its name to his ancestral home leaned against the sky in an ominous pose.

It had always frightened him as a child, when he saw its silhouette propped up against the darkness, and he was none too fond of it now. In his more restless moments, he fantasized about having it pulled down, but it was said to be a relic of a tenth-century monastery that had once stood on the site over which Stonecross Hall had been built. He didn't like the idea of disturbing any further the bones of the long-dead monks who once bent their knees to the cross below.

He shivered, and looked away from the lichen-encrusted monument.

From his periphery, Alaric suddenly saw a flicker of someone moving down below.

There was a person coming up to the great doors laden with parcels, or . . . was it luggage? He frowned, staring harder. Had one of the guests misread the invitation and come too early? He hadn't heard a carriage, and none of the servants were scurrying forth to offer assistance.

Most strange.

The figure came into better focus, and he saw . . . what was it he saw? A strange personage, dressed very oddly. A woman, he thought. The person had a certain gait, an elegant yielding of her figure to motion that could only belong to a female.

Her clothing, from what Alaric could espy from his rather awkward vantage point, was more than outlandish—it was decidedly scandalous. Was that . . . a *bare calf* he saw, flexing beneath her skirts? Even the thought sent a little thrill, like a small jolt of light, coursing through him. The woman's head was equally bare, out of doors in broad daylight, with one of the oddest coiffures he had ever seen blowing in the breeze. He had never seen a lady with shorn hair before—though perhaps the woman (for she *couldn't* be a lady) had recently been ill.

Who was she, and whatever was she doing at his door in such a state of *dishabille*, carrying what could for all he knew be the entirety of her worldly possessions?

Alaric's pulse began to pound erratically. There was something very strange about the figure, something nearly uncanny that had little to do with the eccentric state of her dress. He almost felt as though she wasn't quite there, and it wasn't the distortion of the ancient window glass that obscured his vision. There was something else between them, like a drapery of transparent gauze distorting the air.

Suddenly, the figure looked up at the window, straight at him, and though he had the distinct impression she could not see him clearly through the distorted glass, he could make out her features fairly well, despite the distance. She resembled a watercolor sketch, a swirl of color and form. He perceived the outlines of her straight black brows, elegant as dashes of calligraphy, and her full red mouth pursed in consternation. She was thin as an exclamation point in her loose, rather plain dress. She grew clearer somehow, as if the gauze that had obscured her from his sight had begun to burn away in the moment she looked up at the window. Her dark eyes registered but seemed to look through him, as though he wasn't quite there.

It was a terrible feeling, as if he was shimmering into a state of invisibility as her outline grew starker against the flagstones below. He felt as though his organs must be clearly visible, pulsing within him, his blood a surging tide within tangled veins. His heart leapt against his ribs, a mad animal trying to get away.

He was afraid. He hadn't been afraid in years. He had been far too bored.

Now, he was exhilarated, the inexplicable surge of excitement was headier than any liquor. Who was she, and why was she here? He felt as if he should know her face. He *did* know it, and yet he knew he had never seen it before.

"Father," he said calmly, despite the cold sweat that had broken out on his brow and the jangle of his pulse. "There is someone at the door."

"What?" the old man wheezed, startled awake. He had begun to tire even more easily of late. Alaric was surprised at the number of sensible sentences their conversation had garnered, and though the subject matter was not entirely to his liking, he felt as if he had been given a small and perfectly chosen gift. He strode over to the bed and stroked the old man's hair—a liberty he took only because his father was barely sensate.

"Never mind, sir," he said gently. "I'll make them go away."

He marched from the room, not bothering to close the door, and took the quicker, narrower route down the servants' staircase, nearly colliding with a chambermaid encumbered with a pile of fresh linens in his haste. He didn't know why he was in such a lather to confront a person who made him feel as if he might not exist, a madwoman walking about the countryside in a state of undress. At the back of his mind was the thought that she might need his help. Help that only he could give her. An illogical thought, considering he had helped absolutely no one in many years, least of all himself. He had told his father he would make her go away. He wondered if he would be able—or would even want—to do so.

At the bottom of the stairs, he nearly collided with yet another of the several dozen servants who cluttered up the back stairs of Stonecross—a footman, in this case. He scowled at the young man, who looked suitably cowed by the direct eye contact. "What are you about, Danby?" he demanded. "Do you not know that there is a person at the front door, carrying her own luggage up the walk? I could see her clearly from my father's window."

The footman stared, his impeccable livery pulled slightly askew in his effort to avoid crashing into his master. "No, sir, there can't be! I was only just out there meself. Are you sure it weren't me you saw?"

"It most certainly was not," Alaric said firmly. "I distinctly saw a young woman coming up the walk with several heavy valises. I cannot believe that the members of my staff would be so remiss as to ignore a guest's arrival."

The young man stared at him in open disbelief. "No, sir, I would never do such a thing," he protested. "Honest. There is no one outside."

Alaric strode toward the door, grasping the handle just as he heard the sound of a key fumbling its way into the keyhole.

He frowned. What the devil was happening? No one but the upper members of his staff possessed keys to Stonecross. Alaric himself didn't have a key to the front door. And why would it be locked in broad daylight?

"Allow me, sir," Danby said humbly, gaze averted as he attempted to open the door for Alaric, who shrugged him off impatiently, tugging at the door. It felt as if it had been soldered shut. The brass handle twisted in his hand, as though someone was attempting to open it from the other side, each of them thwarting the other's efforts.

"Just wait a blasted moment!" he muttered, muscling the handle as it shuddered, nearly tearing out of his grasp. Whoever she was, she had a firm grip, despite her willowy shape.

Finally, the door gave way, whooshing inwards as though a wind had pushed it open. Alaric used the momentum to fling it wide, preparing for his encounter with the unannounced, and very peculiar, guest. The mottled October light meandered across the threshold into the dark foyer, barely illumining the polished marble floor beneath his feet.

Alaric immediately began rambling, as he usually did when confronted with a stranger. "Good morning. Please allow my footman to take your things. I am afraid we weren't expecting guests quite so soon—" he said cordially.

To no one.

There was no one there, as Danby had said. The front step was quite abandoned. Fallen leaves strewed the scrubbed stone, and there were no fresh wheel marks disturbing the gravel drive. No one had pulled a carriage up to the house in several days, other than deliverymen, who drove their carts around the back. Alaric stared, baffled.

"Danby," he said. "I swear to God there was a very strange young woman standing not two feet from this spot a few moments ago. What is more, I heard the very distinct sound of a key turning in the lock just as I was opening the door. And as I turned the handle, there was someone on the other side, countermanding my efforts."

He turned to look at the young man, to gauge how Danby was taking what he was saying. To his credit, the footman did his best to retain an expression of polite credulity, but his visage clearly betrayed a more practical sentiment. "Sir," he said, his eyes widening slightly. "Mayhap you don't know it, but there's no key to that door—never has been, as long as I've been here. Mr. Crawley locks up at night and unlocks it in the morning, all from the inside. Once I was locked out on me day off, and I had to sleep in the stable." Danby blushed furiously at that confession, and looked down at his feet, clearly expecting a reprimand. He looked immensely relieved when none was forthcoming.

Alaric stared abstractedly out of the door for a few moments longer, before patting him on the shoulder. "Alright, Danby," he said. "You may close the door. And Danby"—he cleared his throat, glancing sidelong at the flustered footman—"you needn't mention this to anyone. Especially Miss Wright."

"Mention what to me?" Ellen said brightly, wafting into the room in one of her many morning gowns that looked more like confections in a *patisserie* window than they resembled items of clothing. Her hair was elegantly coiffed, her cheeks rosy, and her figure pert. Alaric felt a minute stirring of affection for her that didn't quite bloom into anything more endearing than an appreciation for the pleasant freshness of her complexion. Was it enough? He didn't know.

"That the front door will need polishing and the hinges oiled before our guests arrive," he replied smoothly. "I am afraid the staff has rather been neglecting it of late, and I didn't want to trouble you with it, with all you have to do."

Danby nodded, and bowed, melting away in that singular fashion of servants without needing to be dismissed.

"Thank you, Alaric. That was most considerate of you." Ellen smiled, clearly pleased that he was taking an interest in the party preparations. She took his arm, placing her fingers lightly on his sleeve as she looked up into his face. Thankfully, he had shaved before noon that morning, even though he would only have to do so again before dinner. He wondered idly what Ellen would think if he were to grow the sort of patriarchal beard some sea captains of the region favored. He doubted she would tolerate such an affectation. Facial hair seemed to be the one thing about which she put down her elegantly slippered foot. Indolence and ennui paled in comparison to her aversion to unsightly stubble.

Ellen's eyes shone with the sort of admiration to which most gentleman felt entirely entitled. Alaric only felt unequal to the task of living up to her expectations. He patted her hand absently, his gaze straying again to the door as she began to chatter about party decorations and French desserts. He walked with her into the morning room, which was filled with a watery light. He allowed it to dispel the last cobwebs of unease that still clung to his thoughts.

He had imagined it. That was all.

Clearly he had not been getting enough sleep or exercise. He had been penned up too long in the dreary rooms of Stonecross Hall, which, like all houses of its size and antiquity, was somber at best during the autumn months. Perhaps Ellen was right—a party would do him good.

CHAPTER THREE

In the week following the initial shock of her inheritance,
Laura went on much as she had before, forcing upon her life
at the very least a semblance of the ordinary, with the excep-
tion that she had stopped seeing clients, no longer taking
their meager handfuls of copper gleaned from the week's
housekeeping money.

That part of her life was finished.

Laura was done with the dead.

Taking possession of Stonecross Hall so close to the
end of the month was perhaps an odd way of showing it, as
moving house at All Hallows was thought particularly bad
luck. It meant taking all one's personal ghosts along in the
packing crates, not to mention an open invitation to whatever
other spirits were looking for a home for good measure, but
Laura didn't want to wait to begin her new life. Superstition
be damned.

While she made her preparations, she continued to rise
at her usual time, ate her usual fare, and went to bed with
the cat curled at her feet in her narrow bed. She didn't feel

like an heiress. She didn't feel like anything. She simply went through the motions until the new circumstances of her life began to sink in.

Though she might have given up the flat, she decided instead to keep it. She bought quite a few new pieces of furniture, and new draperies, and had the whole place painted and spruced up. She wanted to have somewhere to return to, and she certainly had the money now to indulge her whims. She could of course buy herself a town house, but she didn't like the idea of rattling around on her own in one of the big, ostentatious London homes of the nouveau riche, a member of which she now undoubtedly was.

Laura hadn't had much style lately, and she certainly wasn't a vulgar woman. She had become rather modest since the war, and wore things that were well made and practical. She was tired of it, tired of her respectable dowdiness, and decided to go on a whirlwind shopping spree, using her new-found wealth to treat herself to a little glamour. She bought new clothes at Harrods, a shop she had never before frequented, and had her hair done. She was positively vampish now, with her marcelled curls, lacquered fingernails, and smoky eyes. Wearing costly French perfume simply because she could, she felt like a girl in a cigarette ad, impossibly chic and untouchable. Laura found out at twenty-eight what those born wealthy already knew: style could be bought and wrapped up in elegant little parcels, delivered right to one's front door. What surprised her most was that she rather liked it, the elegance and utter freedom money allowed. If she wasn't careful, she could easily grow used to wealth. There was an impetuous streak in her that she had almost forgotten in all the postwar doldrums.

Laura also bought a train ticket to the coast of Devon. Stonecross waited there for her. She could see it in her mind's eye, clinging to the treacherous coastline like a stone dragon in a tale of valor.

She told no one she was leaving. There was no one to tell. She posted a notice on her door, stating that she was on holiday for the foreseeable future, and asked her neighbor, old Mrs. Malachy, to keep an eye on the flat for her while she was away. She wasn't worried. Even after she had made her improvements, there was nothing much worth stealing in her pokey little abode. Still, she would miss it. She would miss the sounds wafting up in the small hours from the nightclub down below, the colorful arguments of the drunken clientele as they spilled out each morning into the dawn before returning to whatever unknowable lives they led in the brightness of day. She felt an odd sense of loss, leaving her occasional midnight companions behind. Strangers as they were to her, they were the only people with whom she had shared any real part of herself. Even if it was only a wordless pain she could never express, she could see in their eyes that they knew it well. Now there would be no one. She would dance and drink alone.

The train trip was uneventful, the soot and smoke of London falling farther away with each mile as the first-class car in which she sat ate up the track. It reminded her of the war, as so many things did: the compartments congested with boys in uniform, smelling of damp wool and shaving soap, their faces full of jovial apprehension. How little they understood what was happening to them. How little sense it all made. Now Laura sat in comfort, beautifully dressed in a wool travelling dress, her neatly coiffed hair tucked into a fashionable cloche. Her hands, folded on her lap, were soft and clean—no longer caked in blood. Her fingernails, once broken off in the flesh of some poor lost cause she had tried to help but couldn't, were smooth and shapely, painted crimson to match her lips. Her hands may be clean, but they remembered the color red, and always would.

After what seemed like an eternity of impatient anticipation as the train juddered into station after station, Laura arrived in the little village of Cropton-upon-Moor, a quintessential English village the like of which she had rarely visited, and usually only saw on picture postcards set out in shops for the tourists. Even in the gloom of October, it was picturesque. Laura liked it right away. It made her feel safe, like a child tucked up in a warm, soft bed.

She hired a car to take her to Stonecross from the station, and watched out the window the whole way, taking in the sight of the endless moorland with its odd crags and outcroppings, dotted with sheep and mottled all over with heather that bloomed in a blazing glory of purple and white. She liked autumn heather best, because it bloomed while everything else was dying. There was something wonderfully defiant about that. Laura thought Dartmoor beautiful, a wild, stark sort of grandeur that took her breath away. The endlessness of it was slightly unsettling for a city girl who rarely set foot in the country, and she hoped she would not find it oppressive after the initial novelty wore off. If she felt a twinge of apprehension, Laura pushed it firmly aside. There was no turning back now, unless she wanted to walk the winding country road back to the village, where she would wait two days for the next passenger train.

Laura forgot all of her trepidation as Stonecross came into view.

She stared at it, transfixed. It was monstrously beautiful, its edifice of stone stitched together from varying time periods, from Norman to Elizabethan, with a few Georgian flourishes in the shape of unnecessary Grecian-inspired columns. Whatever she had dreamed or imagined about Stonecross Hall, Laura hadn't expected to fall in love with it. It wasn't the sort of building that easily inspired tenderness. Even in her dreams, it had always made her uneasy. And yet, she had always returned to it, again and again. It hadn't felt like a choice—it felt like an assignation. She *wanted* to be with the house, as it wanted to be with her. It was filled with ghosts, and Laura had always been one of them. And now, finally, she was here, in the flesh, to take up residence in the very real and very unearthly ruin that was what remained of Stonecross Hall.

She still couldn't quite allow herself to believe that it was real. But here it stood. She had a strange sense of dread roiling in the pit of her stomach that was not completely unpleasant. Dread was rather her natural state. She wouldn't know what to do with herself if she felt easy in the world. It was all so bizarre, this sudden change in her fortunes, which had always been middling at best. It still made no sense. What kind of a man was this Alaric Storm III, who had left her the entirety of his fortune, on top of his moldering pile of stones, before she had even been born, or thought of? How could such a thing be? And yet, it had all come through as though it was only marginally unusual. The money was safe in a bank account to which she held the book. The deed was in her name. She was leaning out the car window as it pulled up the drive, the brisk, salted wind tearing her new hairstyle to pieces as her abandoned hat lay uselessly in her lap.

The driver deposited her in the drive, and turned the car back to town. He had seemed inordinately keen to be on his way, barely stopping long enough to hurl her valise and train case rather unceremoniously from the boot before scarpering. She was on her own, with only her pile of luggage and the pile of stone for company—and, of course, the cat, who had meowed piteously in his basket at intervals the whole way down from London. He had no desire to leave his city, and Laura would have left him to his own devices, but at the last moment, she couldn't part with him. He was her only friend. And she didn't want to be entirely alone in the house. Even she needed some form of company when the light dimmed and the fire banked low.

The house itself was exactly the way it had always appeared in her dreams, though somewhat more dilapidated. Sometimes, when she dreamed of Stonecross, it had been little more than a skeleton. At other times, she dreamed of a living house bright with lights, music spilling from the windows, the shouts of laughter and giddiness palpable. Almost too palpable, with an edge of hysteria. It was as though all the lives that had ever been lived there had overlapped, and created a fever pitch of nostalgia. Yet, in all her dreams, she had never seen a single living soul in the house. When she walked up the steps and pushed open the heavy doors, the house was as sullen and empty as a tomb, swallowing her into itself. The interior of Stonecross in her dreams was a terrible, endless void—it was like she was falling forever, blind and voiceless.

Nevertheless, she was always compelled to enter—as she was compelled now to pick up her luggage and struggle as best she could up the cracked stone steps to the wide front door, which sagged sadly on its lintel. Laura also noticed that a great many of the mullioned windows had been broken over the years, and no one had bothered to repair them. She felt fortunate she had the means to do so. She suddenly felt an overwhelming desire to see the much-abused house restored to its former glory, though she supposed it was rather mad to do it for herself. She was just one woman, with no family whatsoever—what did she need with such an alarmingly huge home? She would need to shut most of it up to live in it. She would require staff: gardeners, scullery maids, those sorts of people. And for what? For whom? It was utterly absurd, this notion of her actually *living* in Stonecross. And yet, she longed for it. The house itself longed for it. She could feel it.

Just as she was about to approach the front door, Laura felt absolutely compelled to look up to the second story, where she saw the vague, watery outline of someone in the window, seeming to peer down at her. A ghost in the daylight. She shivered, and took hold of herself. She should be used to such things. Ghosts followed her wherever she went, after all. But this ghost seemed to have been waiting for her. Waiting for who knew how long, biding its time as the walls and windowpanes of Stonecross Hall fell in around it. She saw it as though through a shimmering fog, and her apprehension wavered. She couldn't see it clearly, but it seemed to have a human shape, and human curiosity to go with it. It seemed . . . *alive*. Which it couldn't be. Unless there was someone in the house—which there *couldn't* be. Mr. Tisdale had assured her that no one had been in the house for years.

Laura blinked a few times rapidly, and the apparition melted away, as if stepping back from the glass. It was very possible that her nerves had got the better of her, though they rarely—if ever—had done so before. She had always been steady and levelheaded, even after the ghosts had come to stake their claim on her. Stonecross had already been a part of her life back then, before she and Charles had become orphans and had been sent to live with their grandmother in Cheapside.

Their lives with Grandmother Dearborn were so cheerless that even Stonecross was a sort of haven. Her dreams would take her there, and she would run through its sunlit, eerie halls as free as a little deer in the wood. It was the first time she understood that sunlight did not dispel terror, any more than terror was wholly unenjoyable. Rather, she found she *liked* being terrified. It was a feeling so pure, so deep, that everything else quite paled in comparison. Stonecross was both her worst nightmare and her deepest wish fulfilled. It was with her in every season, at any time of day or night. She need only close her eyes, and step into her dreams, like Alice through the looking glass.

Reaching to unlock the massive double doors, Laura held her breath as she fumbled with the heavy key, the cat beginning to growl in an undertone from the depths of his basket. She ignored him as she tried to wrench the handle, but it was stuck fast.

Almost as if someone on the other side was holding it closed.

Or trying to open it, too.

Laura cleared her mind, checking to see if anyone was there—just in case—and she had a fleeting sense that there *was* someone on the other side of the door. She sensed only someone tall, a man with obscured features. There was still a sense that something diaphanous was between them, through which she could not see in the way she ought to be able to. The man was pulling at the handle. She could feel his presence, a deep vibration surging through the brass to which they both held fast. He was pulling as hard on the door as she was. But what right had he to be pulling on her door in the first place? She felt nothing sinister from him, and there was a flash of a face. Handsome, quite young—seriously annoyed. She sensed his feeling that she had no business there, and yet, he was deeply curious about her. She laughed. What a preposterous life she led. It was just her luck to have the lingering spirit of a long-deceased butler as a welcoming party. She would have to send him on his way, unless he was prepared to be useful. He was, after all, her only staff member at present.

In all likelihood, it was not actually a spirit. It didn't *feel* like one. This intruder felt very much alive, and completely intent on keeping her out. Steeling herself, Laura put her shoulder against the door and pushed with all her might until it finally gave way, no doubt sending her unwelcome visitor flying. She hadn't thought about what she would do when she finally confronted him, a woman alone with nothing but a set of luggage and a trussed-up alley cat to protect her from who knew what sort of ruffian. She drew herself up with every available scrap of hauteur, brandishing her iron key like a blunderbuss and giving her best impression of a barbaric war cry in case the invader's ears were sensitive to shrieking. Her voice rang out like a cracked bell.

Except there was no one there at whom to shriek. Laura could see that much before the door slammed shut behind her with an enormous *boom*. The cat yowled piteously, sensing himself abandoned. Laura struggled with the door again, and dragged her belongings into the foyer. The cat wrestled with his wicker prison as Laura bent to untie the latch.

"Alright, you silly old thing," she said, releasing him. "Go see what you make of the place. And catch whatever mice you find about the premises. You're a working cat now."

The cat sprang free, all of his hair standing on end, his luxuriant tail as big as a bottlebrush. He landed on the very tips of his feet, back arched, his eyes huge as saucers. He stood arrested a moment in an impressive feline pose before tearing off down the length of the darkened foyer, hissing and spitting all the way. He disappeared from sight, and Laura laughed, jumping a little as her voice echoed around her.

Laura sat down a moment, to gather her wits after the strange performance on the stoop. She perched on the edge of her valise, her feet, in their brown leather peep-toed shoes, crossed at the ankles, which were dainty, pretty things the color of good bisque porcelain. Laura was distinctly conscious of them as she admired the straps of her shoes in an effort to distract herself from the racing of her heart. It really was so pleasant to have nice things again. She hadn't in so long. She hadn't bothered. For some reason, she felt like bothering about such things now. As if in confirmation, she caught a faint and delicious whiff of her perfume wafting up from her new frock as she smoothed down the rumples. She felt rather pretty today. It was a good feeling, though there was no one to see her but the ghost, if that was what it was—though it behaved as no ghost Laura had ever known. It was so strong, so real. Perhaps the ghosts of Stonecross were simply more virile than common phantoms.

Laura stood and walked into the bright shafts of autumn sunlight that streamed in through the many broken panes of glass, illuminating the black-and-white checkered marble floor of the foyer. Every surface was covered in the detritus of countless autumns. The skeletal remains of the leaves crinkled beneath her feet, turning into dust, their loamy fragrance drifting up to Laura's nostrils. It was so beautiful, her house, even in the throes of its decay.

The enormous double staircase loomed, and the crystal chandelier swayed and glimmered in the light, though it badly wanted a good cleaning. She would have to get a troupe of maids in, just to take the grime off of everything. There was a statue dominating the center of the foyer, but Laura couldn't see what it depicted, swathed as it was in layers of voluminous sheeting, which had long grayed and had begun to rot. Here and there, hints of a pale limb showed through: a buttock, the curve of a shoulder, a mottled breast. She amused herself with trying to guess its identity, but Laura didn't uncover it. She didn't really like marble statuary. She found it unsettling, the way the sightless eyes always seemed to follow her mournfully about as she moved. She even felt they were looking at her when she was out of sight. She would leave the statue covered, she thought. And then perhaps she would have it taken away.

Laura walked up one side of the staircase and down the

other, looking with interest at the faded ancestral portraits staring with stately gravitas from their chipped gilt frames. She didn't mind portraits so much. At least they depicted people who had lived and died, people who had once been real. She was much more comfortable with them than with marble statues, which were so far beyond anything human. She felt, looking at the portraits, that they could, in time, become old friends of hers, despite their smug expressions. She wondered, as she looked, which of the illustrious gentlemen was her benefactor, Alaric Storm III. None of them looked particularly benevolent.

Perhaps Alaric Storm was nothing of the sort. No doubt he had reasons of his own for what he had done for her. It still didn't sit quite right. It made no sense, an inheritance bequeathed to her before she had even been born. She was of no consequence, her family decently middle class but of no account. She had no relatives, close or distant, and yet, she had inherited an estate and all the wealth needed to see it returned to its former magnificence. The only thing that made her feel as though it was in any way a reality was Stonecross itself. It was hard to ignore now that she was standing in it, despite the supernatural way it had come to her night after night, taking over most of her dreams since she was born. Was that a premonition, or was it something more? She wished she knew.

When she came to the end of the portraits, at the bottom of the second stair, she knew she had found him. Something inside of her, the part of her that always knew things it couldn't possibly know, recognized her long-dead benefactor. What surprised her most was how young he was, how handsome. He had the sort of face that fascinated—Laura was mesmerized. The waves of auburn hair of old-fashioned length clinging to his turned-up collar, the fine, well-shaped brow and long, prominent nose with its equivalent jaw and chin. The full, sensuous mouth that seemed to be frowning even as it smiled. The deep, piercing eyes that were as bright and warmly amber-hued as they must have been on the day the portrait was painted—as they must, no doubt, have been in life.

She felt an overwhelming sense of having *known* him. His face seemed as familiar to her as her own—more so, even. It was odd. A silly fancy. After all, since the ownership of the house had come to her, she had spent so much time imagining him that he had been real to her long before she'd arrived. And his house was even more familiar than he was. Perhaps she had dreamed of him once, without remembering it. It was possible. Everything *was*, after all. Laura had long understood that.

The interesting thing about him was that, unlike the subjects of the other portraits, he was painted in regimentals. He must have been a soldier. Laura felt an immediate deepening of sympathy for him. He knew what it was like, then, to have been caught up in a war. She thought hard for a moment, trying to remember her schoolroom history lessons. Which war would it have been? Not the Boer War . . . the Crimean, perhaps. Unless he was simply a soldier with no war to fight, as so many fortunate people had been, for whom soldiering was a profession, or even a lark, a commission bought for them and then sold when the shine was off of the scabbard.

But Laura thought not. She looked at the young man for

a long time, and she could see in his face an expression all too familiar. It was the expression of one for whom life had lost much of its luster in the aftermath of terrible conflict. No one who hadn't experienced something similar could ever understand. Laura did—more than she wished to. She wondered what he would think of her own experiences as one whose business it had been to sew back together what a bayonet had rendered asunder. Would he think her a fellow comrade, or just a hanger-on, as some people thought of the women who served on the Front, driving ambulances and pushing men's guts back into their abdomens? There were no medals for those like her, no monuments. There never had been.

Transfixed by the portrait, Laura thought again of the man she had sensed pulling at the door. Had it perhaps been the ghost of Alaric Storm himself? She hadn't seen him clearly. She had been, if not afraid of him, then alarmed. And surely a house this large and this old was home to an entire regiment of ghosts. If it *was* Alaric Storm, the question had to be asked: was he trying to keep her out, or invite her in? The peculiar thing was that Laura had been nearly convinced that the man who struggled with her at the door was no ghost. She had really thought him alive, an intruder in her house. She did not get the sense that he was dead. She knew the smell of the dead, the touch of their hands. The man at the door had seemed more alive than many men she had met since the war ended, but that was not really saying very much. Most of the men she had met were ghosts in all ways but one.

Laura walked slowly through the rest of the house as though enjoying a pleasure garden. As the day moved on, the light failed by degrees until she was left with only shadows for company as she explored the labyrinthine corridors. She came across room after room, gallery after gallery. A library, a billiards room, more bathrooms than she could count—only a few of them fitted up with running water, and not a lick of electricity in the whole of the mansion. She found a supply of candles and some matches along the way, and filled her pockets, lighting each candle from the dying wick of the last, as if chain-smoking.

She never seemed to find the same room twice. Each one was eerier and more antiquated than its predecessor. Laura had never seen such opulence, except in her dreams. That was the strangest part. The rooms were exactly as she had dreamed them, time and again—rooms enough to house each of her dreams, it seemed. Some attempt had been made to protect the furniture, but the elements had still penetrated. The lavish silk draperies, bed hangings, and wall coverings had, in many cases, simply rotted to shreds. The sea air was stealthy. It crept in with fingers sleek and damp, leaving nothing but moldering decay. It seemed almost vindictive, like it had some ancient blood feud with the very stones and rafters of the once-great house.

Finding her way back to the foyer at last, Laura stood again beneath the portrait she believed in her soul to be Alaric Storm.

"Who were you?" she whispered to him, staring into the eyes, which seemed to see her, as though some part of the dead man's soul was still contained within the impression of paint. It was the only image of him she had found in the house so far, and she wondered how closely it resembled the actual living man. "What have you to do with me? Why did you leave me this house? And what do you expect me to do with it?"

Alaric Storm III did not reply, though the way the candle-light wavered across his face gave him a certain wry look of amusement that seemed to say, *Why don't you try finding out for yourself?*

She shivered a little, rubbing her arms. It was cold in the house. She could hear the wind keening through the broken windows, could feel its fingernails pressing into her flesh through her dress. She could hear the sea throwing itself against the cliffs, and smell its pungent, bitter perfume. It was the smell both of life and of death, swirling together—a morbid scent. She liked it. Why had no one ever thought to bottle it? It was a scent she would wear for the rest of her life. Though she liked her posh French perfume well enough for a lark, she didn't really like the idea that any woman could smell just like her for the price of a bottle.

Laura took her candle, and wandered back up the stairs to the third story, where the family bedrooms were situated. She had seen one to which she had taken an instant liking, and decided it would be her own. After getting turned around several times, she found it again. She hadn't bothered bringing up her luggage; she would do that in the morning. For now, she would sleep in her slip.

She put the candle on the bedside table, on which she found a quaint brass candlestick of the sort she imagined Ebenezer Scrooge might carry while trying to fend off Marley's ghost. She knew how the old fellow felt, though Laura had long ago given up fending off ghosts. She simply lived with them, and found them much better company than a lot of

people she could name. Stonecross lent itself particularly well
to Dickensian references; all day long she had been expecting
to bump into Miss Havisham in her moldy wedding gown, or
stumble upon her loamy feast in one of the dining halls.

The bedroom Laura chose for herself was in much better
condition than many of the others. It was spacious, with high
ceilings and heavy mahogany furniture that looked like it had
been constructed in the days of the Virgin Queen. The bed
was so high she would need to take a running leap to get into
it. The bedclothes, though musty, were at least intact—a rich
and beautiful blue brocade embroidered with gold. Laura
had always preferred blue in a bedroom. Blue made dreams
deeper, she found, rest richer and more satisfying. She lit a
few more candles and saw to her satisfaction that there was
in fact a fire laid, by some long-dead chambermaid, no doubt.
In fact, the whole room had the hushed air of readiness about
it that felt, so many years later, like a mausoleum. It felt as
though it had been made over in loving tribute to someone
who would never return.

It was a deliciously unnerving feeling, and Laura's skin
began to prickle as she lit a spill and touched the flame to the
kindling. The wood was very dry, and the flames sprang up
almost instantly. She added more wood to the fire, and soon
it was crackling merrily. She would soon be warmer than she
needed to be, so she took the opportunity to throw back the
draperies—carefully, as the silk was quite fragile—and open
the windows. The panes in this part of the house were not
broken, only crazed all over like old porcelain. The hinges
screeched in protest, but Laura managed to muscle them
open. She leaned out, her elbows propped on the windowsill,

and caught her breath in wonder at the sight that spread itself before her. The vast expanse of the roiling sea glimmered in the moonlight, and the stars had come out in all of their glory, shimmering in the deep blue night like spilt sugar. This was not a sight one ever saw in Piccadilly. It wasn't a sight one saw anywhere. It was unique to Stonecross. No wonder the Storms of the past had chosen to build their ancestral home here, on this seemingly inhospitable crag of Devon rock. Laura would have done the same, had she needed an ancestral home of her own.

She decided to leave the windows open while she slept. The air was magnificent. She felt like she was breathing, really *breathing*, for the very first time. Unbuttoning her dress, Laura slid it down her shoulders, letting it fall to a pile at her feet. She didn't bother folding it. She could wear a fresh frock tomorrow, though heaven only knew how she would clean them after she had worn them all. She hadn't thought very practically about that sort of thing, since she had come from London, where she had done all her own washing. She supposed she could do it again, if it came to it. She wasn't fussy about what sort of work she did. After all, she wasn't a lady, despite her surroundings. She snorted. She would *never* be a lady.

Sitting before the mirror at the dressing table, Laura picked up the brush, which sat in a layer of dust. After blowing it clean, she began absently to brush her hair, which was unruly and tangled from the road and her many hours of exploration. She hadn't looked at herself properly in a long time. She tended to avoid a lengthy toilette—an old habit left over from her nursing days, when she barely had time to do more than wash the worst of the blood from her hands and face before donning a fresh cap and apron. She had become very stalwart, all of her vanity burned away in the heat and mess of the battle hospital. She hadn't felt much like a woman in a very long time—and certainly, there had been no one to treat her as such. She hadn't been out with a fellow in years. It was sad, really. And it was not an uncommon lament. She really had no right to complain. At least she had not lost a lover.

Though in a way, she had. She had lost whatever lover she might have had in the war, as surely as she had lost her brother Charles.

Laura had long felt as though the man she was destined to marry was dead, had died before she had the chance to meet him. That was what war did. It killed life's possibilities, until one was left with the dregs. Rather than live that way, Laura had decided to live alone. She was lonely, though. That was the hardest part. She often thought she should find some decent man, some wounded soldier, perhaps, and make him a kind wife. But she didn't really want to be some man's sweet and silent wife. She wanted passion. She wanted love. She wanted a man who *wanted* her. So few of the men who had returned seemed to want anything, and she certainly could not see herself with a man who had not fought. It seemed to her that there would be something essential missing, a sort of joint, generational understanding. No one who hadn't been on the front line could fully understand her. She needed a man who knew what it was to live with ghosts.

Laura looked at herself critically for the first time in years. Usually she simply focused on one portion of her face at a time—at her lips, say, while she slicked on a layer of lip rouge before going down to the dance hall beneath her flat. Or her brow, as she plucked a stray eyebrow. She never looked long into her own eyes. They were far too penetrating, even for her. They were large, deep and dark like pools of liquid ink, and there were always deep shadows beneath them, not to mention the telltale lines of the careworn creasing the corners. Her lashes were thick and full, however, and she had a certain mysterious something that men had responded to, once upon a time.

She smiled at herself, and her cheek dimpled, just as it did when she was a girl and had smiled more easily. She ran her fingers lightly over her face and smoothed the skin of her throat, beneath which the jut of her collarbones was extremely prominent. She was too thin. She had never really gained back her full weight after the war. At the time, emaciation was inevitable. Now, it seemed as though her body didn't truly believe that she had come through, that it could come out of hiding and reinflate itself. She would have to try harder, eat richer foods. She could certainly afford it.

She laughed suddenly. Food. She hadn't even thought to eat any, though she had stashed a few things in her train case, including some tinned fish for the cat, who was still nowhere to be seen. No doubt he would slink into her room sometime in the small hours, his belly rumbling and his fur sleeked back down. Laura wasn't really hungry, and it was too much of a nuisance to go down into the dark house and find her way back again. She wouldn't bother. She would stay right here. Though she wished she had an apple, at the very least. Then she could play one of the games she had when she was a girl.

A laundress's daughter who had lived on her street had told her how, if an unmarried girl cut an apple across its equator so that the seeds made a five-pointed star, and then ate while gazing into a candle set before a mirror on Halloween night, it would show her the face of the man who was to be her husband. There were a lot of folk superstitions to do with that time of year. Laura had never put much store in them, but it was fun to do silly things like that when the moon was full, or All Hallows Eve was approaching, as it was now. Sleeping with an apple under the pillow was said to have the same effect. Such things were best done near midnight, and it was nearing that mysterious hour.

Though she knew she should go to bed, Laura was restless. Despite having no apple, she felt like playing parlor tricks like the ones her grandmother discouraged, perhaps because she knew all too well what Laura was and what she might conjure from the beyond, if given any encouragement at all. There was one other trick she could try, something very similar to the apple trick, except that one only needed to brush one's hair while staring into a candle flame reflected in a mirror. She was in just the right sort of mood to try it. Dreamily, Laura picked up the brush again and began to run it through her hair. The first time she had done it as a child, she had fallen asleep. The second time, during the war, she had seen only a horrible nothingness, dark and palpable, as though the man who might have loved her had never been born, or had died before they could meet.

After the war, she never tried the mirror game again. By then she understood all too well the answer to that particular riddle.

It wasn't that she dozed off, exactly. It was more that she went into a sort of trance. Laura began to stare fixedly into her own deep black eyes, in which the twin flames leapt and wavered, drawing her in. Suddenly, it wasn't her own eyes she saw anymore, or her own face. It was his—pale in the firelight, the room around him the same, but clean, neat as a pin, inhabited.

He was as fascinating as his portrait, his face a series of strong, patrician lines. His eyes were deep-set, with a sweep of darkly golden lashes that contrasted with his slightly coppery hair. There was an understated cleft in the chin, and the stubble that darkened his jaw was the same golden copper as his lashes, though his finely shaped brows were dark auburn, like his hair. The man was dressed in a dark silk dressing gown tied at the waist, beneath which he was naked, his smooth chest strong and rippling. His skin gleamed in the candlelight, lightly burnished. Laura raised her hand to touch her face, and in the mirror, he did the same, his expression giving way steadily to an astonishment she could feel reflected in her own expression.

"Who are you?" she said, though she knew. And his lips mouthed the same words back to her. "What do you want?"

The man in the mirror shook his head sharply, and Laura felt her own head jarred. The impact drew her back to herself abruptly. She was alone in the room, her own familiar face staring dazedly back at her from the age-spotted mirror.

She whirled about, her eyes darting around the room, but it was the same musty, dust-ridden apartment it had been only moments before.

"It was a dream," she said aloud, her voice echoing slightly. "It must have been."

Shaking her head again to clear the cobwebs as she had done in the dream, Laura came away from the mirror. She hesitated, then picked up her frock, and draped it over the glass, so that the mirror was nearly obscured. "There," she said, with satisfaction. "That should keep you on your own side." And then she laughed. It *had* been a dream. She knew that. There were no presences in the room. She would have felt them. In fact, the whole house seemed rather emptier than she had expected. She remembered the strange shadowy impression she had seen earlier, and the strong male presence as she had unlocked the door. She remembered the way the cat had become so hysterical. And then, nothing. Until now.

Perhaps there *was* something here, something residual that she fancied was Alaric Storm, simply because she felt a sort of fascination with him because he was handsome and young in his portrait, and she was young, too—and lonely. So she played the mirror game, and saw his face. But perhaps that was only her fancy. It was a very old house. No doubt there were all sorts of human echoes wandering about the place. Spirits had to have somewhere to go, after all, and not all of them made it to the afterlife. A great many of them preferred to stay right where they were.

Perhaps Laura would do the same, someday.

Perhaps she, too, would take up residence as a ghost of Stonecross, and join Alaric Storm in his midnight rambles.

She shuddered deliciously, like a child with an electric torch pressed beneath its chin, and leapt into the great bedstead. She scrambled beneath the counterpane, and the sheets were cold and clammy. Laura lay awake for a long time in the dimness of the room, listening to the sea crashing and the wind gusting, watching the fire bank itself to embers that glowed in the dark shadows like a hundred leering eyes. She really was the most morbid creature, she thought to herself as she drifted off. She really needed to find some new hobbies. Ghosts were all well and good, but they did make one rather odd. And yet, she thought of Alaric Storm as she drifted off, and his face seemed to brand itself on her eyelids.

CHAPTER FOUR

It only happened because he was tired, had too much to drink at dinner, and couldn't stop thinking about the woman he had seen at the door. The woman he thought he had seen, that was. No one else saw her. She was clearly a figment of his imagination. And as such, it was only natural that he would imagine her again.

He was sitting at the mirror, combing the snarls out of his own hair after having waved Jeffries off to bed. And he was thinking about her. The woman in the strange dress, with the hairstyle that was stranger still. And those *eyes*. She had eyes that had seen too much, more than a human being should. Alaric knew the signs all too well—he saw them now, in his own face. The candlelight flickered over his features, and he seemed both infinitely old and impossibly young, as if every version of himself through every stage of his life were all present at once. And that was when it happened.

He looked into his own eyes, mesmerized by the way the light reflected there seemed to eat them up, obscuring his face so that he began to look like quite another person entirely. Alaric squinted, pushing the illusion further. It was the strangest impression, born entirely of light and shadow. Or so he thought. Until the hair he saw in the mirror began to change. It grew shorter, fuller, curling just beneath earlobes that were far too delicate to be his own. And they were pierced with tiny pearls!

His eyes widened.

He was not looking at himself at all.

This was no trick of the candlelight.

He was seeing some other person entirely. It looked very much like the same woman he had imagined earlier, only now he could see her so much more clearly. And she was barely dressed. She wore only an unusual sort of lacy shift, which displayed the soft swell of her breasts to rather fine effect. Her eyes were large and so deeply brown they were nearly black, fringed with thick lashes. Her mouth was full and ripe, like early cherries drooping from a stem. Was that lip rouge she was wearing? Scandalous. He had always rather liked the effect of lip rouge, though no lady he knew would ever wear it. Clearly, she wasn't a lady.

"Who are you?" he said to the woman in the mirror, indulging the fancy as far as it would take him. To his astonishment, her lips mouthed the same words back to him, perfectly synchronized. "What do you want?"

What on earth was he doing? He must have had far more wine with his dinner than he realized. He was hallucinating. Clearly this was a hallucination. Alaric shook his head briskly, as though to shake the image from his mind's eye, and the woman in the mirror did the same. He squeezed his eyes shut, and when he opened them, blinking, she was gone.

She was gone, but he could smell her perfume. It clung to the darkness like wet silk, and suddenly he was aware that he was *hard*—painfully erect beneath his dressing gown.

He wanted her, badly, and she didn't even exist.

She was built entirely from his own disturbingly potent fantasy.

Was she the sort of woman he craved, instead of one like Ellen Wright, who was any other man's idea of perfection? He tried to think of Ellen now, in all of her flawless grandeur. Her porcelain complexion and rosebud mouth. Her artfully arranged coils of hair the color of summer wheat. Her impossibly tiny waist swathed in layers of silk made up in the latest Parisian *mode*. Her guileless green eyes staring up at him. Then he imagined taking her into his arms, and crushing all of that perfection against him until it was a ruin of silk and linen as he kissed the breath from her body, as he loosened her gown . . .

And he shuddered, the tension in his loins slackening.

He didn't want her.

Not the way he wanted the woman in the mirror with the fascinating face, who could be nothing more than some hallucinatory projection of his own darkest self.

Alaric flung himself on the bed. He stared up at the ceiling, where the light of his guttering candle still wavered, as though taunting him. He tried not to think of her. There *was* no her—she wasn't real. She was no one, a phantom he had conjured because phantoms were the only company he could enjoy. A ghost girl. Where had he even come up with her costume? Was it as simple as wish fulfillment? Ladies *were* damnably overdressed, in his opinion. And that hair, like a secret tangled thicket, the wildness of which was normally only to be found somewhere much lower down. . .

He was hard again.

This time he didn't fight it. He loosened the tie on his dressing gown, beneath which he was naked. He took hold of himself, stroking the length of his cock. He could feel his own pulse throbbing. His whole body pulsed, quivering like horseflesh as Alaric closed his eyes and imagined her in the bed with him.

Her body was like a length of silken ribbon, shimmering in the candlelight, the dark tumble of her sleep-tousled hair falling across her brow. He imagined her in more detail than he had seen in his earlier vision. Her dark eyes drinking him in, her deep red lower lip caught between teeth that were slightly crooked. She smiled at him, slow and sensuous, and a dimple appeared in one soft cheek. The chemise he conjured for her barely covered any of her—she was *not* a demure Victorian debutante. The pale yellow silk clung to her bosom and left her shoulders tantalizingly bare, her flesh the color of fine bisque dappled here and there with freckles. He wanted to taste each and every one of them, run his tongue over ever dip and valley of her lean and supple frame.

As if she really was beside him, he gave into his fantasy completely, swiftly divesting himself of his dressing gown so that he could be naked with her, so that she could see him as he was, stripped of all pretense. He slipped between the sheets, and took the image of her with him.

His fantasy was so real that he let go of himself and reached for her instead.

Alaric slid his hand up the taut length of one sleek thigh,

the curve of her flank swelling into surprisingly full hips. She was both lean and lush, her limbs slender and long and her curves well proportioned. Her breasts pooled over a prominent ribcage, and when he gathered her up against him, he could feel her spine like a string of pearls sliding between his fingers.

It had been a long time since he had been with a woman in this way, and it surprised him that he could imagine a type of body he had never encountered in any of his experiences in the well-heeled bawdy houses of Continental Europe and West London. There was a strength to her, a vitality he didn't usually discover beneath tightly laced stays and frothy feminine linens. When he kissed her, she melted against him yieldingly enough, but her arms and legs seized him in a grip he didn't think he could easily escape, even had he wanted to do so.

And he didn't.

He wanted the fantasy to last—forever, if possible. Was that all she was? Or was she some kind of ghost, coming to life in his arms? No woman had ever felt so real. *He* had never felt so real. In her arms, he was alive for the first time in years.

Laura would never be sure later if it was a dream, though it didn't feel like one at the time. Dreams never did, except in the cheerful, reassuring light of day. And anyway, it wasn't exactly a bad dream. It was pleasant, and uncanny, and extremely sensuous. It was the best dream of Laura's life.

She dreamed she was in the big bed in the blue room, just as she actually was. She lay spread out in the bed, her arms and legs tangled in the rich bedding that smelled like lavender and moss, which was a pleasanter smell than she would have thought. She had the sense that she was just on the cusp of waking, that she drifted lazily beneath the surface of the deep water of sleep and could hear everything around her, all of the delicate night sounds. She could sense the looming edifice of the house cradling her. She was alone. Deliciously alone, and she wasn't a bit afraid.

And then, she wasn't. Alone.

Suddenly, there was the sensation of another person, a presence. A tactile heaviness slid into the bed beside her. She could feel the weight of it pressing down, the whisper of the sheets slithering over naked skin. She felt a hand, touching her, sliding up her body, slowly. Her heart began to hammer, and she tried to cry out, but she was paralyzed. Not with fright. No. She was paralyzed with desire. It was an ache inside her body that seemed to bloom outward, encompassing her, taking hold of her from the inside out. Laura had never felt anything like it before. She tried to open her eyes but she couldn't. She felt the person, the being, whatever it was, touching her all over. He felt fully real, like an actual man made of bone and blood. She could feel his lips at her neck, the silk of his hair falling across her face as he trailed his mouth from her earlobe to her cheek. She opened her mouth as his lips found hers, hot and warm and tasting faintly of cinnamon.

All at once, she could move.

Crying out, she clung to him, wrapping her arms and legs around her ghostly lover. She opened her eyes, but she couldn't see him in the dark. The fire had gone out. The candles she had left burning had been extinguished by the wind from the open window. She slid her hands up his naked back, and cupped his face in her hands, feeling the scrape of stubble on her palms, the sharp relief of his features describing themselves perfectly to her deft fingertips. She knew him. She recognized him as if he was standing before her in a well-lit room.

"Alaric," she said, breathing his name wonderingly.

Who are you? she thought she could hear him say. *How do you know my name?* His voice was like a distant whisper, a child's trick with tin cans and string. When she opened her eyes, she couldn't see him. She closed them again, and he was as solid as she was.

"Laura," she said. "I'm Laura."

Are you a ghost?

She shook her head, laughing shakily. "I haven't even been born."

She felt his unease, and pulled him against her, kissing him, breathing his imaginary breath. She didn't want to tell him that he was the ghost. He was long dead, and yet, here he was in her arms. She was making him real. With her, he would live again.

Much later, when she woke, Laura still felt him there. He felt like a warm, heavy weight on her chest, a penetrating presence holding her down, pinning her in place. She couldn't move. She couldn't open her eyes. When she finally wrestled her eyelids to half-mast, she screamed. There was a pair of eyes glinting at her in the gloom, staring as if they could see into her soul. She laughed. She knew those eyes well.

"You bloody feline!" Laura cursed, shoving him off of her. "Are you trying to crush the life out of me?" He really could stand to lose a pound or two.

Rolling over onto her side, Laura, still smiling, allowed her eyes to come to rest on the vanity at which she had sat the night before, during the first of her strange visions. Well, the first one had been a vision, the second was merely a dream brought on by too much loneliness, a rather heavy feline, and Laura's own hyperactive imagination.

But then, she looked closer. Laura saw that the dress she had draped over the mirror had been flung aside. In the half-light of the imminent dawn, she could see, not her own room, but that *other* room, the perfectly appointed apartment in which her mirror friend had appeared.

Laura blinked her eyes, and the illusion slipped away, but the feeling that something had really happened to her in the night remained. She thought back with mounting unease to her dream, to the bodiless paramour that visited her in the night. Surely it was only psychic noise from her brain, working out some of the leftover impressions the people who once inhabited Stonecross had left behind. Not everything was something. Was it? She didn't know. Usually, she could tell the difference between her imagination and the paranormal. But now, she suddenly wasn't so sure.

She had been so tired lately. She didn't really know what was going on in her subconscious. It was entirely possible she herself had gotten up in the night and pulled her dress from the mirror. Laura often walked in her sleep, and did strange things. More likely it had just slid down to the floor—a simple exercise in gravity. It meant nothing. But more had gone on in the night than the simple removal of her dress from the place she had left it. There had been a presence in her bed that felt much too real to be a dream.

It was all too bizarre, even for Laura, who made her living on the bizarre.

She sighed, flopping back on the pillows. A comical little poof of dust sprung up around her, and she sneezed. And then her belly grumbled. She was *starving*. She hadn't eaten anything at all since the train, and the poor cat must be beside himself as well, after his adventures prowling about Stonecross the day before. She would just creep down and rummage for a bite from her valise. She would really have to think of a way to get some supplies in. She hadn't thought this through at all. She didn't think there was a telephone in the house—or electricity for that matter—or else she could call a grocer in the village and have someone deliver an order of food. Really, she was ridiculous.

Laura threw back the bedclothes and clambered out of bed, careful to avert her eyes from the mirror. Who knew what she might see next. She crept down the back stairs, even though there was no one to hear her. She thought it might be a quicker route. Weren't servants always scampering about great houses like this, using only the back stairs? It must be much more efficient. She really would have to learn her way around.

Halfway down, the oddest thing happened.

Laura smelled the most tantalizing aroma. It was the compounded bouquet of a full English breakfast, including coffee. She sniffed appreciatively, before reminding herself that there was no such possibility. "It's tinned beef and cold tea for you, hen," she told herself. "You've just conjured that smell from pure wishful thinking."

She kept on creeping, and eventually found herself with no more stairs. It must be the main floor. All she needed do was pass through some door or other and she would find herself back in the foyer, where she had left her bags.

That was the plan, at any rate.

Instead, she found herself standing in the doorway of a huge country kitchen.

A huge country kitchen from which wafted the delicious smells that had been driving her to distraction. Not only were there smells drifting out, there were *noises*. Of people *talking*.

"All *I'm* sayin', Mrs. Henderson, love, is that I don't know what that girl is *thinking* of, throwing the master a party," someone said in a huge, booming voice that was only just discernible as female. "He won't thank her for it."

Laura peeked around the corner, her mouth hanging open. She could *see* them, too—a gaggle of women of varying shapes, sizes, and ages, all wearing old-fashioned scullery uniforms with white starched caps and aprons to match. They reminded her of nurses. They had the same sort of brute competency she had seen so often in the more experienced women on the Front.

One of them was kneading a huge slab of dough, picking it up and slapping it down again as if to teach it a sorely needed lesson. She sighed audibly, shaking her head. "You don't need to tell *me*, dearie. I knows what she's like, right enough. And she will have her way, you mark my words. She always does."

"I feel *sorry* for her," piped up another one, a small, scrawny little character, no more than fourteen years old, with a pair of heavy dark brows that nearly met in the middle and a sharply jutting nose far too big for her face. She turned round from her soapy sink to put her tuppence in, spattering the floor with greasy water. "She don't know he won't *never* marry her. She just keeps hoping and hoping, and getting older 'n older . . ."

Mrs. Henderson of the beefy, befloured arms aimed a slap at the girl's rump that knocked her sideways. "Who asked *you*, I'd very much like to know?"

"Tess is right, though," chimed the other, who was cutting sausages from a long string of them. "The master won't never marry, and if he did, it wouldn't be Miss Ellen Wright, for all her beauty and fortune."

"I know she's right, Mrs. Fischer," Mrs. Henderson said in an injured tone. "I just said no one never asked her what she thought! She's a right uppity bit of calico, that one."

Mrs. Fischer nodded judiciously, which seemed to smooth the formidable Mrs. Henderson's feathers somewhat. They kept on gossiping as they worked, while Laura looked on, amazed. "You mark my words," Mrs. Fischer said. "Miss Wright is going to do a *desperate outrage* to herself one of these days. No girl can go on that long, spurned and unloved, and take it like an extra lump of sugar in her tea."

Laura didn't know what to do. The scene before her was utterly bizarre. She had never experienced anything like it. Clearly, she was looking through some sort of . . . doorway. A doorway into Stonecross's past. These ladies were no ghosts. They were more real, much more alive, than she was. She could smell their good, honest sweat mingling with the odors of their cooking. She could taste the silt of flour flying on the air from their workspace to her mouth. It coated her skin in a fine dust. If she wasn't careful, she would—

Sneeze!

It was the biggest sneeze of her life. It was more like an explosion than a sneeze. The three women in the kitchen looked up, staring at her. She could see them through her bleary, watering eyes as she tried to pat her nose dry on the back of her hand. She stared back at them, wide-eyed. Her outburst had arrested both their movements and their talk. It was so quiet, all Laura could hear was the sizzling of the sausages in the big cast-iron skillet on the stove.

She quickly smoothed her hands over the hurricane sleep had made of her once-carefully marcelled curls in an attempt to look respectable. She was sure she only made it worse, drawing attention to the oddness of her hairstyle. Yesterday's mascara didn't help her case any, either. She resorted to standing very, very still, as though they were a trio of deer she didn't wish to frighten. To their credit, they didn't *look* frightened, only curious and slightly bemused.

"Are you lost, dearie?" Mrs. Henderson barked, not unkindly. Laura blushed as the big woman's eyes moved over her person with interest, taking in the scantiness of her clothing.

"The poor child is near naked!" Tess, the little dish skivvy squeaked, though she was many years younger than Laura, a veritable child herself.

"Did you need something, Miss?" Mrs. Fischer inquired decorously, with an awkward curtsy. "Only, guests usually wait in the dining room for breakfast, see."

"And they usually have more clothes on," Mrs. Henderson muttered.

"I . . . I'm dreadfully sorry," Laura stuttered. "I couldn't wait."

"The poor child is *famished!*" the skinny little maid said.

"I am, rather," Laura said lamely.

"Well, hurry up, and get her a tray!" Mrs. Henderson bellowed, taking another swipe at the girl. "What, were you born yesterday? I'm dreadfully sorry, Miss! If we had known, Tess here would have brought you a tray."

"Oh, no! Not at all," Laura said humbly. "I'm so sorry to have bothered you."

"Not at all, not at all. Tess! Look lively, girl, before it goes stone cold!"

Tess hopped to it, putting a cup and saucer filled with hot tea on a tray with several sausages, a boiled egg, and an elegant silver rack full of buttered toast. She danced nimbly over to the doorway with her burden.

And then she gave Laura a look that was so utterly penetrating that it seemed to reach past her heart to grip her spine. The girl's eyes narrowed, her thick black brows crashing together in consternation. Gone was the little skivvy shrieking meaningless commentary as she hopped about the kitchen like a scalded hen. In her place was a girl as uncanny as Laura herself, with eyes as old as any she had ever seen. Tess had knowing eyes, eyes that *saw*. Laura stared back at her, utterly paralyzed. *She knew.* She knew Laura didn't belong.

"If you'll just tell me which room you're in, miss, I'll meet you there right quick," Tess said, in a normal voice. But her face told a different story. *I see you,* her eyes seemed to say. *You have no business here.*

"Oh, no!" Laura said quickly, trying to remain calm. "You

mustn't dream of it." She held out her hands, her heart hammering as Tess laid the tray carefully in her hands.

There was a faint tingling sensation that was oddly unpleasant as Tess's fingers brushed hers. The girl continued to gaze at her in that unnerving way, and Laura trembled as she took the tray. Her eyes dropped for a moment, to make sure the dishes she held were steady before she trusted her grip.

"Thank you, ladies," she said with as much brightness as she could muster, looking up again. "You have been most kind—"

She nearly dropped the tray when she saw that the kitchen was completely deserted.

It had been for some time. Decades. There was a thick carpet of dust over everything. The few pots that remained hanging in place had dulled to a deep verdigris. Broken crockery was scattered everywhere, and there was a fusty smell that reminded Laura of the loamy perfume of graves. She looked down to the tray she held in her hands, and though the silverware and dishes she had been given were all there, they were cracked and crazed with age—and completely empty.

Laura dropped the tray with a crash, and fled back up the stairs.

She wasn't afraid. She was *not* afraid.

She was terrified.

CHAPTER FIVE

Laura roamed through the corridors of Stonecross, purposefully getting lost in an attempt to calm her mind and return herself to a state of reason. The rest of the house seemed perfectly normal—that was to say, a complete ruin, the way she had left it before her expedition downstairs. Though the kitchen was a little worse for wear after Laura added her own personal touch to the detritus when she dropped the tray of dishes to the floor. Now there were shards everywhere, and some of them happened to be pieces of Laura's own mind. She had never felt crazy before, not during any of her séances. Not even on the Front, when her hands and gown were drenched in the bloody gore of some poor boy's insides. She had always been calm, utterly detached, until she went to sleep at night, and the dreams came to lay their horrible hands on her.

Now, it was the opposite. At night, her dreams were sweet, sensual—heavenly. Stonecross was still a part of them, but the war was not. The trouble was, when she woke, the visions went on. And she didn't understand where they were coming from. She had seen ghosts before, it was true. But these ghosts were different. The kitchen women weren't sad spirits straying into Laura's realm, reaching out to her with beseeching hands. They were complete beings, busy living their lives, completely unaware that anything more than moderately unusual was happening. Except for the little one. Tess. Though she played the part of the frazzled underling before her superiors, she had looked at Laura with such wise and knowing eyes. She looked at her and knew she didn't belong. Not in Tess's world. And perhaps not in her own.

And it was true; she didn't belong in her time anymore. It had been destroyed. Laura and every member of her generation were orphans in time. Part of the reason she longed for Stonecross so much was because of the visions it had shown her of another time and place, a gracious, opulent era that dazzled her senses. Perhaps some part of her believed that living there would bring that feeling into her life. With enough money, she could restore Stonecross to its former time and glory, and then live as a guest in the mausoleum she had made. No doubt her psychic sensitivities had been amplified by actually being in the house, and somehow she was seeing more than she usually was able to see when in contact with the dead. After all, Stonecross belonged to them. From inside of it, she was able to see into their lives, to the point where she had been half-convinced the morning before that Alaric Storm himself had being trying to open the front door for her.

And then she had seen him in the mirror.

And then, had somehow lured him, bodiless, into her bed.

But was it his ghost she had seen and felt, or was it something else altogether, something outside of her experience?

Her mind reeled, turning over and in on itself, until she felt seasick. She raked her hand through her unruly hair, which hadn't seen the business end of a brush since the night before and badly wanted a wash and set.

She had paced all the way through the third and fourth floors, and the glint of a dressing-table mirror in one of the bedrooms brought her up short as she walked by. She stood and stared at herself, eyes widening. She started to laugh, throwing back her head and leaning against the door frame.

She looked like an utter and complete harpy. No wonder Tess and her colleagues had given Laura strange looks. It wasn't only that she was barely dressed; she looked like a hurricane had carried her off during the night. Her hair was a tangle of whorls and ringlets, standing straight up on her head in places. Her eyes were rimmed in shadow, thanks to her failure to wash her face properly before going to bed. Her lipstick had stained her lips in a fairly pleasing manner, but she didn't think the staff of Stonecross in whichever era Tess lived were used to ladies who wore cosmetics. Laura had little doubt that she had resembled, to their shrewd eyes, someone approaching the status of a streetwalker, or an equally disreputable woman of the stage.

Her mind strayed to the activities in which she had been engaged during her sleep, and she blushed, though there was no one watching, and no one who knew the things she had dreamed. Or about whom she dreamed them. It was just like her, to dream about a dead man with desire. Laura laughed again, and shrugged defiantly, as if in answer to some invisible detractor. She had long been ravaged by ghosts. Perhaps it was time she was ravished by one. She replayed every delicious sensation her unseen lover had teased from her skin. The silken heat of his mouth in such thrilling contrast with the rasp of his jawline. The memory of the way he had clasped and caressed her gave Laura gooseflesh, as though he was with her now, about to touch her again. She imagined him kissing her, his tongue teasing the sensitive seam of her lips until they opened like the heart of a rose. Laura could almost taste his breath, laced with cinnamon and fine whiskey . . .

She gasped, and shook her head. She was becoming brain-addled again. She would come to her senses once she had freshened up. It was, after all, her own room she had stopped at without realizing it. It was more than time she tidied herself and got dressed, in case she startled an unsuspecting ghostly chambermaid. Though whatever clothing she chose was sure to raise a Victorian eyebrow or two, at least she would have decently combed hair and a scrubbed face.

She didn't realize straightaway that anything was different about the room when she entered it. If she registered the oddly pleasant tingle that crept over her bare skin as she crossed the threshold, Laura was too distracted to blame it on anything more paranormal than a chilly draft. She walked over to the washstand, upon which stood a very convenient ewer of water, and splashed some water into the basin. She leaned over and began scrubbing her face with the bracing liquid, and had begun to pat it dry with a fresh flannel before she understood what had happened.

She hadn't brought any water up to her room. She was going to get some when she went down to the kitchen for breakfast, but then she had fled before she could.

Laura looked into the mirror in front of her, and saw that

it was not in the least marred by the years it had sat unused. It shone as brightly as if it had only been polished an hour before. She stared into her own wide eyes, her face stripped clean and pink, her freckles showing like they had when she was a school-girl and had yet to apply her very first dusting of powder.

Behind her, the bedroom in which she had slept had taken on the aspect of a previous incarnation. The wallpaper was fresh and bright, the carpet free of the destruction moths would wreak in decades to come. The windows sparkled where they peeked through the beautifully arranged drapes, open just enough so that a single shaft of light illumined the bed. It was made up in the same linens and spread beneath which Laura had dreamed the night before.

Beneath which, in Laura's place, there now slept a man.

Alaric. It could be no other.

Laura's breath caught in her throat. Her heart began a painful timpani—it felt like an animal scrabbling to get out. She swallowed it back down and crept across the carpet to the bed, her bare toes curling in anticipation. She touched the bed with the tips of her fingers, trailing them over the lush blue brocade that felt fully solid beneath her hand. The man beneath it stirred, and her heart leapt back into her mouth, but he didn't wake. He lay on his back with one long arm flung out and the other cradled behind his head, the smooth muscles flowing into a rippling expanse of shoulder.

This was the man who had set her dreams on fire. She felt as though she had already memorized him, as if she had been born knowing his face.

Laura leaned closer, drinking in every inch of him with her eyes.

The delicious curve of his lower lip had softened in his sleep amidst the gleaming copper stubble that stippled his jaw, and Laura longed to trace it with her tongue, marking his lips as hers. The prominent nose with its aquiline contour. The fan of golden eyelashes glinting like feathers of gold. Tousled auburn hair clung to his brow, curling down the length of his long, taut neck. His skin was warmly hued, not like the skin of most red-haired people she knew. It was like living bronze, only paler, minutely freckled. Only a lover could ever have seen the texture of the golden hair that grew over his forearms and dusted his finely molded chest.

Jealousy washed over her in a seething wave as she wondered how many women had seen him in a similar state of undress. She wanted to erase every trace of them from his golden skin. It had been marked enough already. She could see that he truly had been a soldier. Scars hatched his flesh in random places, all of them faded nearly back to the same shade as his skin. None of them marred him in her eyes, however. Each faded wound only served to deepen the affinity she felt for him.

Affinity.

What a perfect word. It described what she felt for him and what she felt for Stonecross so succinctly, she need never use another.

She reached out reflexively to brush the hair from his brow, but she couldn't touch him. It was as if she was made of water. Her hand seemed to part around him, or go through him. She couldn't tell which. Tentatively, she placed her hand upon the counterpane where it covered his abdomen, her touch light as air. She could feel the shape of him, but she knew that if she pressed too hard, her hand would simply slip through him, though she had a feeling the bedclothes would remain solid. She remembered back to the moment when Tess had laid the laden tray in her hands. For a moment, their fingers had touched, and it felt so peculiar. Perhaps they hadn't touched at all. Perhaps they had simply intersected, like random shafts of light.

Laura touched her fingers to her cheek. She had washed her face in Alaric's basin, and dried it with the towel she had found there, no doubt laid out for him by one of the chambermaids. When the apparition faded, would she find her skin as badly in need of a good scrub as it had been before? What were the rules to the things that were happening? Clearly, she could touch anything inanimate—anything that could still exist in her own realm as well as his. If she pressed too hard when touching him, would her hand grasp right through his flesh to catch hold of his eternal bone? For surely his skeleton must rest somewhere. That part of him was still with her in her own world, whereas no part of her could be with him where he was. So how could she even be standing here? It was all too impossible. She didn't understand it.

At that moment, Alaric opened his eyes.

Laura's own eyes widened at the sight of them, heavy-lidded with sleep. They were beautiful, like smooth cabochons of Baltic amber blinking in the single beam of light. Laura couldn't breathe. She couldn't move. Not even when he smiled with infinite sweetness, clearly able to see her, and reached out to take her wrist in his hand. She sensed only an oddly thrilling pressure that made her feel as though her bones were melting. He was reaching right into the core of her, and setting it on fire. Laura was no longer flesh and blood, but a torch, burning.

"Hello, Ghost Girl," he said, his voice more than the murmur she had deciphered in the dark the night before. It was low and deep, hoarse with sleep and last night's whiskey. She felt it in the stem of her spine. It climbed up her back until she could feel it stroke her neck, as tactile as his fingers against her skin were not.

"Am I dreaming again?" he said, when she didn't reply.

Laura opened her mouth to speak, but couldn't make a sound. She shook her head, and then tried harder. "I don't think so. Unless I am, too."

He smiled again, and she wasn't certain he believed her. He sat up, pulling her toward him. And she went, though she didn't think he could really have coerced her if she didn't want to go to him.

As if she ever wouldn't. At this point, he could lead her off of the cliff over which Stonecross was perched, and she would barely hesitate before composing her body into her very best swan dive. It was a strange thought, and she shivered, pulling away from him slightly. Her mind was turning wild again—dangerous. Laura had had such thoughts before, but she had always managed to turn them back. Many of the girls who worked on the Front felt that way at one time or another. War did things to women, things it didn't do to men. The genders seemed to suffer in separate hells. She wondered if she wasn't a touch mad beneath her seeming composure. She had never thought so before, but coming to Stonecross was changing everything she thought she knew. Now, she knew *nothing*—and *felt* everything.

Laura looked at Alaric's hand holding fast to her forearm. It looked strange, like he really was holding on to something inside of her. To some part of her more real than anything she could see.

He looked at the place where they touched, too, his face taking on an expression of bemused disbelief. "Are you certain we're not dreaming?" he said.

"I'm not certain of anything, Mr. Storm," she said as lightly as she could.

His eyes widened. "You *do* know my name. I thought I had dreamed that, at the very least. Does that mean that your name really is Laura?"

She nodded. "It is. Laura Dearborn. Can you . . . feel me?" She tugged her arm slightly, and his hand seemed to slide through her, until he held nothing but empty air.

"I feel . . . something. Like . . . a sort of vibration that feels solid until I press past it, as if you are made up of molecules that move only just fast enough to make you seem real. I've read of such things." He looked at her almost sternly. "*Are* you real?"

"Yes. As real as you are," she said, laughing shakily. She trembled all over. She felt cold in her extremities. She didn't quite feel as certain as she sounded. "I'm just not . . . *where* you are. Or rather, when. At least, that's what I think."

His brow furrowed, his amber eyes darkening. "This is extremely odd. I wonder if I might still be asleep."

Laura came closer, pressing her thighs against the bed. She reached out to trace his cheekbone lightly. She could feel nothing more than the vibration he spoke of. "Do you wish to wake up?" she asked in a tremulous voice. "For me to go away, and leave you in peace?"

In wordless answer, he closed his eyes, and attempted to press his cheek against her palm. He turned his face, nestling his lips against her palm in a slow, searing kiss she wanted very badly to be able to feel. He reached for her and gathered her essence up, gently urging her to climb up on the bed.

She did as he wanted, straddling him cautiously. The crumpled yellow silk slip she still wore rode up over her pale thighs, and his eyes caressed the curves of her body the way his hands could not. All he need do was look at her, and she was naked before him, stripped utterly bare. Not physically, though that would be wonderful. It was a different sort of nakedness, one she had never shared with any of the men who had been her lovers. She could barely remember them now, here with him. He made every single man she had ever known slide from her memory like darkness from the light of day.

She placed her hands lightly on his shoulders, careful not to put any more pressure on him than she had to. Though it looked as though she was really touching him, it was a pretty illusion, one she would take in place of the real thing if she must. She had no other choice. When his hands grazed the lengths of her naked thighs, she leaned forward, as though to nuzzle his neck.

She could smell him.

The rich musk of his sleep-heated skin rose to her nostrils beneath the scent of his soap, like bergamot and oakmoss, and a hint of the lavender that kept his linens sweet. She recognized it as the scent that clung to the sheets she slept in the night before, as though Alaric had only just risen from her bed. Or had just slid into it. She had experienced that before, in dealing with spirits. They often left spectral scents behind to enchant the living into a false state of connection.

But the man whose scent enthralled her now was no specter. No more than she.

Laura closed her eyes as his hands continued their exploration, sliding over her hips and up her back. She was imagining the dream she'd had the night before, when he was bodiless but tactile. A vision conjured purely from her own mind. The mind was so much more powerful than the body. She could almost believe that the things he had done to her in her sleep were real, even though it was clear to her now that they couldn't touch each other. She had *felt* him, though. So completely. She had almost been convinced that he had felt her, too, from within the great yawning chasm of Time that had somehow closed for a moment, sealing them inside a temporal bubble, together but apart.

As if reading her mind, Alaric murmured, "It seemed so real last night."

She leaned back, breaking his hold on her. She felt his hands ripple through her as though she was indeed made of water. "Last night? You mean, you were . . . with me?"

Alaric flushed crimson, squeezing his eyes shut like a chastened schoolboy caught dipping his sweetheart's pigtails in an inkwell. "I . . . was imagining you," he said, smiling guiltily. "While I was . . . *alone.*"

She felt heat rush over her like wildfire.

He had been thinking about her in an intimate way, and the potency of his thoughts had somehow awakened a response in her subconscious mind.

"What time was that?" she asked, just to be sure.

"About midnight," he said. "After something very bizarre happened in my dressing table mirror that I don't like to mention. You will think me mad."

Laura nodded, blushing madly. "I was there. That was . . . a game I was playing, that a silly girl taught me when I was young. Are you telling me it was real for you, too?"

"It was the strangest thing I've ever experienced," Alaric told her. "My face changed in the mirror. It melted into yours. I thought I was imagining it. I thought you were a fantasy. And that was why I . . . continued. Fantasizing."

Laura laughed, covering her face with her hands. Alaric tried to pull them away, and she let them slip down until she was looking him in the face again. "After that, I fell asleep at about midnight. Like you, I was alone. And then, suddenly, I wasn't. You were there with me. Touching me. Like a lover."

He stared at her, shocked into silence. In his eyes, Laura could almost see every touch and caress he had lavished her with replaying in his mind. He groaned, and raked his hands over his face. "God, what you must think of me!"

"Alaric, you did nothing I didn't want you to. I'm no shrinking violet." She made an ironic gesture at the tableau their bodies had made on the bed. "As you may have guessed by now."

"I didn't know that you were . . . real. Unless I have finally gone mad, and this is yet another figment of my addled brain."

Laura traced the outline of a particularly brutal scar, a reminder of the things that had tormented him. Though he couldn't see them, Laura had scars of her own. "I understand that feeling," she said softly.

He shook his head. "You cannot. No woman can."

"Perhaps not in your time," she said. "Though I think Miss Nightingale would disagree. I assure you, Mr. Storm—many of the women of my generation understand your pain all too well."

He studied her with deepening interest, and something like respect, as though she had confirmed something he had suspected. "Will you tell me about it?"

"Sometime, if you like," she said lightly, grazing his chest with her fingernails. Though he couldn't feel them, his flesh quivered, rippling beneath her hands. "Although I can think of much more diverting pastimes."

His mouth twitched into a smile. "Pastimes that would only drive us mad, as we cannot feel their effects."

"We did last night," Laura said.

"Yes, but how?"

She shook her head. "I don't know. It must have been a psychic connection that had nothing to do with . . . whatever is happening now."

"That sounds shockingly like Spiritualistic claptrap. Table turning, and I don't know what nonsense."

Laura raised an imperious eyebrow and gave him a sound thump on the chest. A blow that went right through him, though he gasped, laughing. "It *isn't* claptrap. I happen to be a psychic medium. Which is no doubt how all of this is even possible. So mind your manners, sir."

He raised his hands in mock surrender. "My lady, I do apologize."

"I am not a lady."

His eyes raked over her, sending a delicious tremor through her gossamer form. "So I see. And I am heartily glad. Ladies are not generally my favorite species."

She dropped her eyes, looking up at him through her lashes. "Do you have one of your own?" she asked softly. "A lady, I mean."

He flushed again, and opened his mouth to speak.

Just then, there was a smart, albeit diffident, knock at the door. Laura's heart gave a great leap, and she sprang from the bed just as the door swung open, her knees and elbows raking through his chest and thighs as if he wasn't there. She dove for the curtains just in time.

Chapter Six

Alaric's eyes were huge with alarm as he scrambled to prevent his transparent guest from leaving, but she darted behind the draperies before he could catch hold of the hem of her chemise, as if he could use it reel her back into his arms. Which of course, he couldn't.

"Just a minute, damn you!" he barked as Jeffries backed into the room, carrying his breakfast tray.

"As you say, sir," the man said, impervious to his master's tone. He stood, waiting, while Alaric leapt from the bed in a tangle of sheets, nearly losing his balance and breaking his damned neck in his fever to catch the slippery minx of his waking dreams.

He disentangled himself and tore back the curtains.

There was no one there. Only the weak sunlight of another dreary October day greeted him as he stood, naked, his chest heaving. She had disappeared. And God only knew if he would see her again. He inhaled, and smelled only the faintest exhalation of her scent.

Alaric dropped his hands, standing disconsolately for a

moment, staring at the spot where she would have been, had she been made of flesh and blood. She swore she was as real as he was, but that was no comparison. Alaric hadn't been real for years.

He turned around, reaching for his dressing gown. He drew it slowly over his feverish skin, and belted it at his waist. "Alright, Jeffries," he said. "Bring the tray."

As though he was an automaton freshly wound and springing to life, Jeffries reanimated and came briskly to Alaric's side, laying the tray down on the small table beside the fire. He drew the battered wingback chair Alaric insisted was his favorite nearer to the modest repast, and set about stoking the fire back to a blazing roar.

Alaric flung himself into the comforting bulges of his chair, and began to pick dispiritedly at his meal, which was light and continental when he wanted something greasy and comforting, a repellently *English* breakfast. He would have to venture down to the dining room for that, where the sideboard would be laden with kippers, crisp bacon, and crumpets. And the table would be laden with Ellen.

He decided to stay where he was. He was never up to facing Ellen's bracing morning cheerfulness much before noon.

Jeffries poured him a cup of wickedly strong tea laced liberally with sugar and lemon, the way Alaric liked it. He drank it greedily. "Ever see a ghost, Jeffries?" he said conversationally, after the singular elixir had begun to perform its restorative magic.

Jeffries did not so much as pause in his meticulous ministrations. "I cannot say that I have had the displeasure, sir," he said dryly. "Unless one counts raising sir up from the dead after one of his nightly trysts with the brandy decanter, which, of course, I do. So, yes."

Alaric stared at him, open-mouthed, before chuckling appreciatively. "I had no idea you possessed such a thing as a sense of humor, Jeffries," he commented, with a snort. "You might have informed me earlier. Make no such lapse in future, and perhaps we might have a lot more fun around here."

"Yes, sir," Jeffries replied with customary blandness, though Alaric thought he detected a minute twitch at the corner of the middle-aged man's thin mouth that signalled he was in a high good humor indeed.

At least someone was.

Alaric was feeling distinctly wrung out after his bizarre rendezvous. Though it was odd how easily one accepted the fantastic when it was happening. The aftermath was the difficult part, when he was alone again, with only a lingering scent of clove-kissed jasmine to convince him that he wasn't irrevocably mad. Almost, but not quite.

After Jeffries left him, Alaric sat with a second cup of tea cooling in his hand, and thought. He thought until he no longer knew how. About Laura, the girl he had conjured, as surely as she had conjured him. She was a self-confessed Spiritualist, but what was his excuse? Crippling lust and loneliness? Was that enough to bring a woman from some unimaginable future into his arms? For she had talked about her own time as though it was someplace far off, where women were different, as she so clearly was different, from the women he knew. It wasn't just that he wanted a woman half-naked in his bed and so had imagined her that way. She had a whole separate culture and custom from the one he knew. Even the way she spoke was different: there was a cadence to her voice that had nothing to do with class or geography. She was a different breed from him altogether. If he searched the world in which he lived, high and low, he would never find a woman like her.

If she hadn't been born yet, as she had claimed the night before to his utter disbelief, then that meant that in her time he must already be dead. He was the ghost. And Laura? What was she? Alaric didn't know. A soul. A future human being. The polar opposite of whatever he was.

All he knew was that he wanted to know her. A few fleeting moments in which they were both barely present wouldn't be enough, any more than marrying Ellen would be enough. He wanted a woman who fascinated him. He shuddered to think of how his life would be when Ellen had him in hand, like another one of her elegant and fashionable possessions. A husband was always *de rigueur* for a lady of the *bon ton*, even if he was dead inside.

But he needn't be dead inside. Something was waking in him, a coiled dragon of desire and longing that must now be fed if he was to remain unconsumed. If he didn't find a way to feed it, the beast would turn inward and feast on his re-kindled heart.

Alaric rose, and rang again for Jeffries. He would dress before noon today, for a change.

In the days that followed, Alaric began to spend more time with his father. It soothed him, somehow, and he thought the old fellow liked seeing him, though he didn't always know who his son was. Alaric didn't mind. He didn't always know, either. He hadn't spent much time with his father since his illness began. Guilt ate at him because he knew he could never summon back the years of neglect. He wasn't a very good son, but he could try to make up for it, in part, before the final moment came.

Alaric the Second liked to be pushed about in his invalid chair, a great, rickety monstrosity with a trick wheel that had seen better days the century before. Only Alaric seemed to have the knack of shoving it around the grounds without upsetting it every few minutes. The nursemaids bundled his father up in several dozen layers of clothing, including a bizarre knitted hat, covered him from toe to chin in woollen blankets, and peered anxiously from the front windows the entire time the pair spent ambling about. They made quite a matched set: Alaric the younger with his game leg, and Alaric the elder with his withered limbs. But it was nice. Alaric thought the air did his father good, despite the cautions of staff, who seemed to believe every disease known to mankind was airborne and intent on infiltrating the stalwart mullioned windows of Stonecross Hall.

They followed the sea path along the very edge of the grounds, and Alaric pushed the chair as close to the cliff as he dared, leaving several meters of space. When he was a child, he used to stand as close as he could without falling—his toes bare inches from the precipice—while Ellen and his sister Lizzie screamed at him to come back. He loved to frighten them. He loved to frighten himself. Perhaps that was part of why he went to war, to live in that state of mania that made the blood burn in his veins. He had always been foolhardy, full of masculine pride and daring. And he had paid dearly for it. He stayed well away from the edge now. His balance was not at all what it used to be. He couldn't be to throw himself backward if he slipped.

"Ellen never liked coming out here, even as children," he remarked to his father, whose rheumy eyes were gazing intently out at the hazy expanse of the water. "She likes water only in controlled doses, at Brighton, or Bath."

"Ellen was a pragmatic child," his father wheezed. The fresh air seemed to rouse him to a reassuring state of alertness. He was having a good day, perhaps one of the few he had left. "She hasn't changed. She knows what she wants, and always has."

"Wanting it doesn't mean she will get it."

The old man shot him a look. "Is there any reason why she shouldn't?"

Alaric sighed. "None that would make any sense."

"Marry her, my son—and soon. I want to see you settled before I die. Ellen will be a good wife to you, and really, that is all one may ask of any woman."

"Is that all you wanted from Mother?"

"Your mother and I had a model marriage, God rest her. It gives me a great sense of peace to think that I will soon be joining her."

Alaric crouched down on his haunches, stretching the stiffness out of his bad leg. He didn't like towering over his father, who had once been such a tall and striking figure, taller than Alaric by several inches. He had never quite managed to catch up. "Did you love her, Father? Were you in love with her?"

"We didn't make such distinctions in my day, lad. We were fond of each other. We shared a mutual respect and admiration. Our marriage was considered the most successful of our generation. You should be so lucky as to make a similar arrangement."

"I know I should feel that way," he muttered. "But I can't seem to feel the things I should. Not for Ellen. Not for anything, really."

"I don't think you try hard enough, Alaric."

"No. Perhaps I don't. And I can't seem to want to do even that."

"Marriage is a civil agreement between two parties with mutual goals," his father said with a sigh, trying another tack. "Ellen wishes to marry to secure her position in Society, and to be the mother of children who will care for her in her age. You wish to secure an heir for Stonecross, and to be taken care of the way only a wife can care for a man. There is no more reason to delay such an arrangement than there is reason to delay breathing. It's as natural as that."

Alaric nodded. "I know. I know it is, Father. But I can't help wanting something . . . more."

"What more do you think there is, my son?"

"Passion. Mutual fascination. Desire. I want to choose a wife because she is the only person with whom I can be myself. Is that so wrong?"

"No one with breeding is ever oneself in front of a lady, Alaric. One is oneself before other gentlemen only. Why do you think we go off to our clubs, and out en masse to shoot at things, while the ladies remain at home in the comfort of their sitting rooms with other ladies?"

Alaric sighed. "Father, as I never do either of those things, I haven't the faintest idea, other than that it is because it is the sort of thing we have always done. We men are creatures of such intolerable habit."

"Perhaps it is time you marry Ellen and take her off to London, where you may resume gentlemanly pursuits instead of brooding about like Heathcliff, or I don't know whom."

Alaric laughed, and his father's eyes seemed to smile back at him the way they had when he was a boy, and they had shared a joke the ladies didn't understand. "Father, I had no idea you even knew who Heathcliff was."

"Ellen reads to me in the mornings, while you are laying about in bed, sleeping off your whiskey. She is very kind to me, though I don't follow half of what she says."

Alaric looked for a long time into his father's face, which was seamed all over with many lines and furrows, each of which he could trace back to one of his own exploits, if pressed.

"You really wish me to marry her," he said, with a sigh. A single tendril of dread licked at him, spreading from the pit of his stomach. He didn't know why he felt so. It was really quite childish of him. It wasn't as though he was asking if his father thought he might do well with a trip to the gallows, or a rendezvous with the blade of a guillotine. It was only marriage, after all. As natural as taking the next breath, as his father said—not as terrifying as walking in a straight line off of a cliff.

"You will be the better for it, lad," his father promised. "Marriage settles one. Until a man marries, he is little more than a boy. A wife makes a man of one."

Alaric nodded. "Yes. I expect she does, in one way or another."

"Good. Let me know when I may congratulate you and kiss my new daughter."

"I shall, Father. I need time to . . . prepare." He got up, his legs turned to lead beneath him. He took hold of his father's chair and turned it about. "We must get you back inside. I don't like the look of those clouds."

A low, long rumble of thunder sounded as they made their way along the walk back to the house, where the nurses were waiting. A bright burst of light illuminated and then erased the world. He thought he saw Laura for one brief instant, but when the sky returned to its former dimness, he saw only Ellen at the window, raising her hand in greeting, a froth of white lace spilling from her upturned sleeve.

Despite his conversation with his father, he didn't propose to Ellen. He couldn't bring himself to do it. It was as if he became paralyzed every time he even considered it.

Instead, Alaric kept looking for Laura. Behind every curtain, in every stray shaft of light. He walked the grounds, hoping to catch sight of her doing the same. Sometimes, it worked. He saw her crouched among the weeds, tracing a Gothic detail on one of the stone walls with her fingertip. Or he passed her in the corridors, wandering along, examining the paintings and engravings that covered some of Stonecross's walls. Sometimes, when they could, they said a few words, reached out to touch hands.

Once, he hadn't seen her in time, and he walked right

through her. She parted around him like a curtain. He felt a sort of silken, sliding warmth, and there was a roaring in his ears like he could hear her heartbeat, the rushing of blood through her organs. When he spun round, she wasn't there. But he felt her. His flesh tingled as though he was being prodded all over with tiny needles.

One night, a few days after he had seen her in the mirror, Alaric saw her dancing. As he was drowsing in his chair long after he should have gone to bed, he heard an odd, discordant tune. He opened his eyes to find Laura singing to herself, and swaying in time to the tempo. She hummed a few bars and then sang a bit of it in a breathy undertone as she sashayed about, coming into focus. She danced to her music, the strangest dance he had ever seen, full of movement and a frenetic rhythm he didn't think he could ever mimic.

He sat mesmerized, watching her, the coils of her short hair flying about, her shoulders and hips moving in sensuous counter-rhythm. She smoked a cigarette clamped into a long holder, and the plumes of smoke she exhaled swirled about her, as though gathering her in. As they closed over her like a slowly drawn curtain, she disappeared without seeing that he was there, that she had come to him without realizing it. Her eyes had been closed the whole time, and for some reason, he didn't call out. He had simply wanted to watch her, to see her as she was in her private moments when she didn't put on any sort of mask of civility. Like him, she was a wild thing. He could see it in the way she moved. He had never seen anyone move like that. He wanted to catch hold of her just so he could let her go again, and be the one who gave her back her freedom.

Chapter Seven

It kept happening. Every day, Laura had visions of Alaric. She saw him moving about Stonecross, languid and rumpled, glass or book in hand. She saw him through the windows, standing and staring out to sea. Or if she was walking the grounds, she saw him at the window, gazing out. She could never be sure if he saw her. His gaze was penetrating even when he seemed to be looking at nothing at all.

At night, she felt and saw him more clearly. There had been more than one encounter since the night she first slept in the bed that had once been his. She had even woken up on one occasion with him sleeping next to her, but she couldn't rouse him. When she tried to shake him by the shoulder he was little more than vapor in her hands, even though he was as clearly delineated against the pillow as he had been that morning Laura had accidentally stumbled into his room. So she curled up beside him and watched him sleep until he drifted away, taking his bedroom with him. She always seemed to appear in his world. He had never so much strayed a fingernail into hers. And he was always more real, more physically present, at night, after the fire banked low in the grate and the sea began to whisper its nothings in her ear.

Finally, after several days of confusing encounters, she'd had to get out of the house in order to think about what was happening without having her mind clouded with stray visions—if that was even what they were.

It has to do with midnight. That must be it. Midnight and the time of year, she thought as she pumped furiously at the pedals of the bicycle she had found languishing in a garden shed. There was no other even slightly feasible explanation.

With all of the odd activity, it was no wonder she had felt such a burst of energy and a need to expend it as swiftly as possible. The bicycle and the winding country road on which she found herself were excellent cures, though she had briefly considered a dip in the frigid sea before coming to her senses and arranging a slightly less dangerous pastime. And because even she couldn't live on bully beef forever, Laura had decided to make the trip into town, killing two birds with one rickety stone.

The rugged countryside of Dartmoor hugged the road on both sides, and Laura's hair blew about as if she had been caught in a maelstrom. The weird outcroppings of the famous Haytor Rocks thrust up from the moorland to pierce the sky like Neolithic pagan structures. It was wild and beautiful, dotted here and there with tenant crofts and the small distinct white mounds that could only be sheep. Laura felt thrilled from tip to toes to be out in the air after the thick miasma of stink and noise that had always enveloped her in London.

Though she hadn't ridden a bicycle in years, she took right

back to it like the proverbial duck to water. She had oiled the chain and pumped up the tires the way Charles had shown her when she was a girl. He had left his own precious bicycle in her care when he went off to war. She still had it, though she never rode it now. She should. It might make her feel closer to her brother to use something he had once cherished.

She didn't like to think of Charles.

She used to think it was because she was afraid of bringing his ghost back to her, tearing him away from whatever peace he had found. Which was foolish, because she knew it didn't work that way. Though she was beginning to wonder if she actually knew how it worked after all. And now she realized she had been foolish, banishing Charles's memory. He was her brother, and her love for him couldn't hurt her now. Not after so many years. It did him a great disservice, pretending that he never existed. That he didn't exist now, in some other, better place.

Perhaps Alaric was there with him.

For she couldn't ignore the fact that when they weren't together, Alaric was dead, and she hadn't even been born. Not in his time. Which was as good as being dead herself.

The thought sent a knife through her heart, and twisted it. She didn't mind the thought of being dead so much as she minded not existing in the same world he inhabited. It seemed wrong, somehow. Terribly obscene. She was meant to know him. She was meant to be with him. It was the one thing she knew with unshakable certainty.

Perhaps Stonecross had drawn her to it in an attempt to set Fate straight, who must have got her facts mixed up and sent their souls to separate places. Perhaps they were being punished for something they had done wrong in another life. Or perhaps it was a test, and they needed to find a way out of the mess they were in. Many Spiritualists believed such things. Laura had never gone in for the faith-based aspect of her lifestyle. She thought so much of it wishful hokum.

And yet . . . here she was. With no other likely explanation.

The fact was, Alaric had left her his house in his will. That was irrefutable. How could he have done that if he had never known her? It was an endless loop, a Möbius of confusion. When she was a child, Laura had had to make one in school, with a strip of paper and a dab of paste. She had marvelled at the way the seemingly simple loop of foolscap had twisted in on itself. It was her first inkling of infinitude. And now, it was the only thing upon which her mind could anchor itself.

This was happening to her because it had happened to her before, and would happen to her again. It was happening because it could never stop. It might change, certain details might shift and take on a different shape, but the fact that she was here, now, coasting along the road that led from Stonecross to the small village of Cropton and back again, was all it took to convince her that Time was not a straight line. Time was a loop. And it was infinite, so that all moments were the same moment. Going forward was the same as going back.

She couldn't wait to tell Alaric.

If only she knew when she would see him again.

At midnight. She could see him at midnight. Or at least touch him. Would there be a midnight in their future when the two states could at last be combined—the seeing and the touching? Perhaps at All Hallows, when the veils between realms were thin, so thin some said they disappeared. That was why people dressed up in costume: to fool the ghosts and the ghouls into thinking the living were like them, for that one night of the year.

Laura wondered now how many people she had seen in costume as a girl were in fact travellers from another time. Perhaps the fear and wonder she had seen on some of their faces was more genuine than she had realized.

Cropton came into view around the next bend, and Laura peddled swiftly into the heart of the small village. The High Street comprised a handful of buildings, including two pubs, a greengrocer, and a general store, the latter two of which she could depend upon for her basic needs. Despite her recent spending spree, Laura's wants had always been basic. She patted her hair down and entered the general store, aware of the peculiar looks her wool trousers, wellies, and Charles's old raggedy sweater were attracting. She hadn't any other really warm, practical bicycle-riding clothes, and the wind bit through them as it was. She smiled and nodded, and the people nodded back, friendliness overtaking their initial suspicion. *God bless the English country folk*, she thought. *Fair Britannia's staunchest protectors.*

She bought a pound of tea, bread, sugar, a pint of cream, a rasher of bacon, a pound of butter, and a small wheel of soft cheese—thought for a moment, and added a dozen eggs and a sixpence worth of licorice allsorts. It was all she had room for in her basket, which was, luckily, a rather prodigious size, the sort from which French onion merchants hawked their wares.

Laura paid with a smile and a nod, and was aware of everyone staring at her. She wondered if they paid all strangers the same amount of attention, or if they knew very well who she was, where she lived, and why. She didn't know how they could, but she was more than aware of the strange mystical powers of country people, who seemed to know every event that happened in their vicinity, whether of great or little importance. No doubt her appearance in the shop would provide fodder for chewing for a week at least. She wished her neatly arranged hair had survived the trip, and that she had had the forethought to adorn her scrubbed face with a swipe of lipstick, at the very least. She was aware that she must be quite a disappointment to her new neighbors, who might be forgiven for expecting someone much more fashionable and glamorous in the person of the village heiress.

One old woman threw her a particularly penetrating look, and she looked vaguely familiar to Laura, who didn't usually forget a face. She shrugged it off, tossing the lady a smile as she left the shop, the bells jangling after her. She felt the woman's eyes on her as she walked down the street, but curiosity was a common commodity, and she thought nothing more of it.

After arranging the delivery of her more cumbersome necessaries, and a regular supply of ice for the ancient icebox in the pantry, Laura went on her way. The bicycle, overladen with her supplies, was even more rickety, juddering all over the road, hitting every bump and hollow until Laura felt as though her skeleton was about to rattle right out of her body. She steered as manfully as she could, but by the time she arrived at the picturesque stone church that marked the halfway point to Stonecross Hall, she admitted momentary defeat, and came to a shuddering halt at the gate of the overgrown little cemetery. Careful to balance the capricious contraption against the low wall so that the basket was resting firmly on top of the stones, Laura pushed the rusty gate open. It squawked in protest, but gave way with reasonably good grace. Clearly, no one visited the people interred within very often. And to be fair, it looked like a very old graveyard indeed. Perhaps there was no one left who survived its inhabitants.

Laura rather liked graveyards. They were peaceful places. Once the dead were in the ground and their bodies were at rest, all the bother and indecency of death was neatly done away with. Though their souls were not always so peaceful. Which was where Laura came in. She liked to sit in a graveyard on occasion, to remind herself what death should be like. Quiet. Restful. Final. It was what she hoped for herself, when her time came to that inevitable stopping point. She didn't fear death; she only feared unwillingly living a tedious afterlife.

Wending her way through the monuments, which leaned this way and that, stalwart against the sky as though mimicking their more impressive neighbors, the Haytor Stones, Laura was unaware that she was looking for anything in particular.

Or anyone.

That was what she told herself, at any rate. But she had begun, reflexively, to gather up some of the prettier weeds and more tenacious late-blooming wildflowers that grew along the shelter of the cemetery wall, until she held a bedraggled, but somehow wild and lovely, bouquet in her hands. Her eyes scanned the tombstones, only registering the barest details before discarding them.

And then she found it. In fact, she nearly brained herself running into it.

The mausoleum was large and imposing, with an austere grandeur that mirrored the ancestral home of the people who now dwelt forever within its vaults. Laura stood trembling before it, her little bouquet clenched in her fist, her head bowed as she avoided for a few long moments the name inscribed in perfectly carved letters on the stone: STORM.

Alaric's family. The family in whose home she was now living, though she had no blood right. Her hands fell limply to her side, one of them still clinging to her pitiful collection of weeds as she entered the crypt.

It was huge. Monolithic. Multi-chambered like a vast and complicated heart that cherished only the dead. The stone was plainly carved; no ostentation, just good, firm, clean lines. The interior was surprisingly light and airy, the remains filed away in compartments according to rank. Lesser sons, wives, and daughters of the family Storm on one side, with all of their extended issue opposite. Laura couldn't begin to count them. Fathers and first sons were interred in separate crypts down the center, covered in heavy lids that bore their elaborate epitaphs, unlike their less hallowed relatives, whose compartments bore little more than their names, the dates of their births and deaths, and to which Storm they had been married or born.

Laura walked along the vaults, trailing her hand over each of the Storm patriarchs in turn. There were two Alarics, the First and Second of their name, at the edge of the fifth chamber. And then, in the sixth, standing completely alone, with no son by his side, was the last crypt.

Laura's breath came in jerky gasps, and her eyes blurred with tears as she approached. She didn't want to look. She didn't want to see him that way. But she knew she must. She knew she needed to see her quest through to the inevitable end. She caressed the smooth marble with her hand, unconsciously scattering the posy she had collected over the surface of the simple epitaph:

ALARIC STORM III
BELOVED SON, HONORED HUSBAND
VETERAN OF THE CRIMEA
31 OCTOBER 1835 – 16 MAY 1891

Sobbing, Laura laid her cheek on the chilled stone, her hot tears trickling over the contours of her face in a way they never had for her brother. When Charles had been killed, she went entirely numb. She'd never wept for him the way she wept now for this man she barely knew. And yet, she did know him. She had known no one better. There was something between them that was wordless and vast as the time that separated them. And leaning against his tomb, knowing that his bones rested beneath her hot, wet cheek was more than she could bear.

After she'd had a good long cry, Laura forced herself to stand upright again. She frowned, reading the inscription more carefully than she had at first, inscribing each word on her memory.

Especially those that read *Honored Husband*.

Whose honored husband was he?

Just before they had been interrupted by whichever servant cared for him in the morning, she had asked Alaric if he had a lady. He had hesitated. Laura had no idea if he would have answered her, or if he would have used some sort of evasion maneuver to steer the conversation away from the topic at hand. Had he married by the time Laura knew him? She was consorting with a man sixty-odd years her senior who had been dead nearly ten years by the time she was born. Was she consorting with a *married* dead man at that?

Dead she could handle. It was her vocation.

Sixty years her senior was not really an issue, either, since she had been visiting him in one of his earlier years.

But married was another thing entirely.

She didn't *want* him to be married. She couldn't stand the thought of Alaric belonging to another woman. Even if he was unhappily married. Somehow that made it worse, because it could be the reason he so readily accepted her presence in his world. He was desperately lonely. He was not understood. He needed someone.

Just like Laura.

But Laura needed Alaric in particular. She needed him with everything that was in her.

What if Alaric only needed someone—anyone— even her?

Her stomach filling with the molten heat of dread, Laura whirled about to face the opposite wall, in which the females of the family were interred. And she saw that there was only a single occupied compartment. One woman buried alone in a cold catacomb. Alaric's epigraph said nothing of children. Clearly, he hadn't any. The Storm line died with him, and with his wife.

Laura walked slowly closer, her knees turning to water.

She wanted to read the name. She needed to know the identity of the woman she may have betrayed, in all but the final act.

ELLEN WRIGHT
20 APRIL 1838 – 13 JANUARY 1880
WIFE OF ALARIC STORM III,
LAST OF HIS NAME

Reading it, Laura shivered. There was something ominous—nearly spiteful—in the last line of script. It was as though some fearsome lesson had been taught. A price exacted and paid.

Alaric Storm III, Last of His Name.

Laura didn't like it. She wanted to scratch the terrible words from the stone until her fingernails were broken and bloody. With a cry, she rushed forth, and struck at the place where her beloved had been negated. It wasn't his tomb that erased him. It was his wife's.

In her distraction, she didn't hear the footsteps behind her. She heard only the voice, creaking like the cemetery gate in the Dartmoor wind.

"I've been waiting for you."

CHAPTER EIGHT

Laura spun around, badly startled, her blood roaring in her ears. It was the old woman from the shop who had stared at her so penetratingly, her handsome face crinkled all over like a discarded sheet of paper. Again, she felt the pervading sense of familiarity wash over her as she studied the lady's face—the thick black brows and beak of a nose. The sharp eyes like polished obsidian that seemed to see straight into her. Where had she seen that face before? And why did she feel like it had changed vastly since the last time she saw it?

"What do you mean, you've been waiting for me?" Laura asked, bewildered. "Did you follow me here?"

The woman nodded. "I saw your bicycle leaning against the wall, and I pulled over." She looked about her, bright eyes taking in every detail, both of the scattered flora decorating the lone tomb and of Laura herself, including her tear-streaked face. "If it was anyone but you, I would have been surprised. Nobody much comes in here anymore. Nobody but the birds, the wind, and me."

"If it was anyone but me," Laura repeated faintly. She

looked hard at the woman, who had the temerity to grin briefly, a flash of yellowed teeth. She seemed so familiar and yet, where would Laura have seen her before? It wasn't in the way she looked; it was how she moved, how she spoke, the way her dark brows scrunched together over her eyes that were still clear and sharp, not at all rheumy like those of so many elderly people. She was spry, too, and as she allowed Laura to take a good long look at her, she paced about with sure-footed efficiency.

She ambled over to the opposing wall and peered up at Ellen's compartment, where the lone inhabitant whiled away the afterlife. Laura sidled cautiously up beside her, keeping the old lady within the periphery of her gaze as she, too, looked upon the epitaph, reading it over again.

The woman sighed heavily. "Ah, it's a sad business, the lives some people lead."

"You knew her?" Laura asked, her interest sharpened even further. If the old dame wouldn't elaborate on the cryptic remarks she had made at the beginning of their interaction, perhaps Laura could coax more out of her in another way, talking of other things. Though the dead woman at whose graveside they stood could hardly be less removed from Laura's concerns, and the old woman seemed to know it.

"Aye, I did, right enough. She was a pleasant lady, but a foolish one."

"How so?"

"She married a man what didn't love her, and never would."

Laura's heart sped up, as if riding a bicycle of its own. "That's sad."

"It is, young woman," she said, turning her penetrating gaze sharply back to Laura, who could feel it take hold like minute talons pressing into her. "Nothing sadder in this life. She was married to him"—she nodded toward Alaric's crypt—"and though she was never very sorry for it, she should have been. There's nothing worse than marrying a man fatally in love with another."

Laura's mouth went dry as she followed the old woman's gaze. The tomb was like an anvil anchoring her heart, so that it beat only with great, painful effort. The sight of it fascinated her; she didn't want to tear her eyes away from the place where Alaric's bones had been milled slowly into dust over many long years. The bones that once animated the dead man she had touched with her own living body.

"Who was he in love with?" she asked, because she couldn't help herself. She wanted someone—anyone—else to know it, and say it.

"With you, of course," the old woman said. "And well you know it."

Laura turned to her, staring wildly. "How do *you* know it? Who are you?"

"Look at me, young woman. Peel the years away from my face with your mind, as if paring an apple. See me the way I was, if you can. And you being what you are, I know you can."

Laura's hand crept up to her mouth, and she bit down on the tips of her fingers in a conscious attempt to clear her senses. Was this another apparition, another gift from the deep past? She looked hard at the woman, and a flash came over her: a pair of wide dark eyes, a knitted brow, the strange vibration of fingers brushing through her own. How stupid could she be, she who knew things, who saw what others didn't? Had she completely lost her gift along with her heart, or had she merely been disregarding it? The thought frightened her, and she willed herself to remain calm, to be the woman she was. She wasn't ordinary and never could be. There was nothing whatsoever to be frightened about. She set her mouth, and drew her trembling body up. She stood calm and tall, and became herself again. A woman who knew. "Tess," she said. "The little kitchen maid."

Tess's laughter was like the hoarse bark of an old hound. "Very good, my dear. Now clear the cobwebs from your head, and come with me. We've a lot to say to each other. I've been waiting more than half my life for you to turn up again. *Much* more than half of it, truth be told."

She scampered back out the way she came, her spindly legs swimming in her battered wellies as Laura followed docilely along. The light was dimming, the sky giving up its negligible light as Tess supervised Laura while she stowed her groceries and crammed her bicycle as best she could into the back of the rickety old jalopy that was Tess's means of transport. Laura swallowed nervously, and held tight to her seat with both hands as she saw how the wizened woman's head barely crested the dashboard. Her feet hardly reached the pedals, but she sailed merrily along at breakneck speed, and managed to miss a fair few of the road's many ruts.

After a while, Laura adjusted to Tess's unique driving style, and relaxed a little, though she never let go of her seat. "Where are we going?" she asked.

"To my croft. You've got nothing worth sitting on at that pile of rubble you're living in. I might have known you were mad enough to come."

"I . . . he . . . left it to me. The house. I was compelled."

Tess nodded. "I've no doubt of it. Once I saw the fashions starting to get more and more outlandish after the war, I knew you'd soon be on your way, with your cropped hair and lip rouge and bare knees." She glanced over at Laura's clothing with an appraising gaze. "Though I never did see you in trousers. I rather fancy trousers myself, though they ain't proper for visiting a cemetery."

Laura ignored that remark. "You mean you've seen me more than once?"

"Haven't you seen me? You must have, or else you wouldn't have known me."

"Just once," Laura said. "A few days ago." Had it only been a few days? The strange scene in the kitchen seemed like a month ago. "I dropped the tray you gave me, after. There was nothing on it but old dishes and dust."

Tess nodded. "You dropped it on my end, too, disappearing like a candle guttering. A good thing, too, or Mrs. Henderson and Mrs. Fischer might have made more of a fuss of your disappearing like that. They seemed to forget you as soon as you'd gone, thought you'd legged it back to your room after I dropped toast and egg on your toes." She cackled. "All those dishes came straight out of my wages, and I was sore cross with you, I can tell you!"

"I don't blame you," Laura said feelingly. "I'm dreadfully sorry."

Tess said nothing to that, her smile fading slowly as she veered into a little lane that meandered up to a small whitewashed cottage at the edge of the cliff, not very far at all from the gates of Stonecross. Tess pulled up and parked haphazardly, cutting the engine with a splutter of fumes Laura could taste. They sat for a moment in silence, Laura's hands fidgeting in her lap. She could see into the grounds from where they sat, quiet for a moment.

Laura gazed at the ancient stone cross that marked an earlier Benedictine settlement. It shone eerily, as if beckoning her from a time far more distant than Alaric's. It reminded her that Stonecross was more than a house. It was a whole history buried beneath heather and stone. Dartmoor was covered in these striking stone edifices, most of them marking the path for ancient travellers making their way between long-lost monasteries. Laura knew without having to see them all that this was the most beautiful one. It was the one that led her through the mists back home to Stonecross Hall, as it must once have led Alaric.

"He gave me my house, too," Tess said softly, breaking the silence. "The master did. He always took care of us, right to the end."

Laura shivered. She didn't want to talk about Alaric being dead, but she supposed they must. Everything led up to that inevitability, for every living person. For Tess and Laura, too, though Laura's time was far more distant, God willing. Alaric's time had already come.

She wanted nothing more than to jump from the shabby little automobile, leap onto her bike, and pedal as fast as she could for Stonecross—for home—where she would open every door in the whole house until she found a room with Alaric in it. Alive. Breathing. Full of the life that was still his, somewhere in time. And even though she couldn't touch him, she would crawl right into this living warmth and stay there forever. Or until she faded back away.

"I don't understand any of this," she said hollowly.

The old woman patted her kindly with a gnarled hand. "No more do I, dearie. But it's happening, all the same. Now come inside with me, and I'll make us a nice cup of tea and a bite of something. And we'll do what we can to make sense of things."

The cottage was snug, full of the fuggy warmth of a peat fire. Tess pressed Laura into an overstuffed and antimacassar-covered armchair in front of the hearth. Laura listened to her bustle about in the small, tidy kitchen, filling the kettle and rattling crockery. It seemed like a perfectly ordinary country croft, with a spinning wheel in the corner, a fat cat blinking balefully from the hearthstone, bundled herbs drying on hooks from the low, smoke-stained rafters. Laura sank back, taking it all in with complacent lassitude.

Until she began to notice a few oddities amidst all the snug English pastoralism. A curious little figure on the mantel in the crude shape of a woman, a sort of pagan deity, with unusual runes scratched onto its belly. Some arcane-seeming books on a shelf, with titles that were anything but mundane, including a full thirteen-volume set of *The Golden Bough*. And then there was the battered and well-thumbed deck of tarot cards scattered on the small kitchen table on which Tess had set out the tea things. She didn't think she would have to look hard to find a spirit board and planchette, or perhaps a scrying bowl—the requisite tools of any serious seer.

"Tea's ready," Tess said, throwing Laura a sharp look as she noticed her focused scrutiny. "Ah, well, doesn't it take one to know one?"

Laura looked at her, and nodded. "I knew you were . . . something. Like me. When you looked at me so strangely before I disappeared. Had you seen me before?"

Tess shrugged. "Not like that. But . . . I had felt something. A presence that didn't belong. At first, I thought you was a ghost."

"Am I not, in a way? Not now, but when I . . . appear. There."

"It may seem that way, to those who don't know of such things. There are more things in heaven and on earth, my dear. And you are one of those things. I've always been curious: how did the master take it, the first time he seen you? I couldn't be sure you'd met him yet, but when I saw your bicycle at the graveyard, I knew you must have."

"Yes, he's seen me. Several times. And . . . he takes it surprisingly well. He thinks I'm some kind of fabrication of his own mind."

"Mayhap that's all we ever are, even to those we love most," Tess mused, pouring the strong black brew into a pair of mismatched teacups. Laura drank deep, grateful for its steadying potency. There wasn't much a cup of good, strong tea couldn't fix—except perhaps for a pair of lovers born in separate times. Even tea couldn't help that.

Tess looked at her levelly. "Can you touch each other yet?"

Laura reddened. "No. Not really. Except once, when I was in a trance, and he was . . . thinking of me. But Alaric wasn't physically present. I could feel him, but he wasn't there. And on his side, I was more like a fantasy than anything he could really touch." She reached out and pressed the old woman's mottled arm. "How do you know anything about this?"

"I know because it's happened before, and it will happen

again, forever, until you and the master set it right." She *tsked* impatiently. "Don't you know that yourself? Don't you *feel* it, in your bones, when you're with him? You've been coming here like this forever. How else do you think the master could leave you Stonecross in his will? He leaves it to you because it's what he's always done. He waits for you for the rest of his days, married to a woman he doesn't love, and then he dies, still waiting. I know, because I was there, waiting with him. And I will be again. Unless you do something to change it."

Laura stared at the older woman with mounting dread. "But he doesn't even know he's supposed to leave it to me. He doesn't really understand where I'm from, or why I'm at Stonecross to begin with. I don't think he knows that I'm real."

"Because you haven't *made* him know it, young woman," Tess chided. "You haven't told him anything he needs to know."

"It isn't my fault," Laura said. "It can't be my fault—that he waits for me. I can't stay there more than a few minutes at a time."

"For now," Tess agreed. "But you will get stronger. And you know why."

"Because of All Hallows, when the veils between realms disappear," Laura said, without knowing she would say it. It came instinctively.

"The night of the party, the master's birthday," Tess nodded. "The night he announces his engagement to Ellen Wright. Tomorrow night, sixty years ago exactly."

"But I am not a spirit," Laura said, with a frown. "The same rules can't possibly apply."

"You said it yourself, girl. You *are* a spirit to his world, as he is to yours. He isn't what you are, it's true, and that's why you're the one crossing over. He never will. Not until he really is a ghost. And then I will be there to make sure he doesn't linger." Tess nodded judiciously. "I'd never let a good man suffer much more than he has to. And that's why you aren't blundering into his real ghost, you see. Because it ain't there. Any apparition of Alaric Storm you see is the man himself."

Laura looked at her with wonder. "If all this is true, what do you expect me to do?"

"Stay with him, of course. You don't belong here anymore. Surely you can feel that."

Laura could. There was nothing left for her here but Stonecross, and she wouldn't lose it. She would have it as it was meant to be, whole and living, a true home the like of which she had never had. "Stay with him," she said slowly. "And stop him from marrying Ellen."

"And ruining both of their lives, as well as yours."

"Until I came here, I thought it already was ruined," Laura said tremulously. "And then I met . . . him. And I knew he was mine, and that I was his. But it's impossible, isn't it? Surely I can't stay there."

"You don't know until you've tried."

"How do you know I haven't tried already?"

"Because if you had, this wouldn't be happening now. Everything would have changed. Time itself would have changed, and we would never know any better."

Laura's mind reeled. It made sense, and then again . . . it didn't. Back and forth. The Möbius twisting. The serpent eating its own tail. She pressed her fists to her temples, and squeezed her eyes shut. "What if he doesn't believe me? Damn, I hardly believe myself."

"Make him," Tess said.

Laura reached reflexively for the scattered tarot deck. It felt off-kilter to touch another medium's cards, and her hands shook, as if resisting the terrible imposition she was forcing them to enact, but she compelled herself to shuffle, over and over again, until it felt right.

Tess watched her silently. Though she sipped her tea calmly, she looked like a carrion bird waiting for the leftovers of another creature's kill.

Finally, Laura stopped. She cut the deck three times, and then turned over three cards.

The first card she chose was The Lovers, reversed.

The second was the Wheel of Fortune.

The final card was Death.

Past, present, and future were laid out before her. She knew if she had her own deck with her, she would draw the same three cards. She studied them, biting her lip until she drew a bright bead of blood. It slid from her lip, landing with an audible *plop* on the Death card.

Slowly, she rose. A sense of absolute serenity came over her, the sort of certainty she hadn't experienced since her days as a nurse, in those moments when she had known absolutely what must be done, and how to do it. "I know what I must do," she said, as if she needed to hear it aloud.

Tess nodded. She leaned forward and gathered up the three cards. She handed them to Laura. "Take them. To remind yourself."

Laura took them, putting them in her pocket. "Goodbye,

Tess," she said, with a smile as meaningful as she could make it. "If all goes well, you won't see me again."

"But you'll see me, young woman. Depend on it. Don't let me give you any trouble, neither. I was a right impudent little scrap of calico in them days."

Laura nodded. She reached impulsively for the old woman's hand, whose grip was unsurprisingly fierce. "Thank you."

She crossed the room, opened the door, and went out. There was just enough of the disjointed autumn light left to see her way home to Stonecross before darkness took her.

CHAPTER NINE

The first day of the house party was the single longest and most boring of Alaric's life.

Guests—invited for the weekend—had arrived in droves. They pressed in on him from all sides, filling up the guest rooms, spilling out from the drawing rooms, parlors, dining hall, ballroom, billiards room, library, conservatory, and every other usable room with which Stonecross was furnished. Alaric mingled amongst them, playing the gracious host with a radiant Ellen never straying far from his side. He could see what she was about: making sure the two of them seemed like one impenetrable unit, already joined in spirit if not in fact. Though she had no understanding what such a bond meant. Ellen thought husbands were little more than fashionable accessories, at the least. At the most, they were symbols of status, equally valuable and as inanimate as the ropes of glittering diamonds she displayed to full effect against the creamy, untouchable backdrop of her beautiful neck.

He thought of Laura's neck, unadorned but for a series of beauty marks much lovelier than any string of pearls, no matter how costly. There was nothing pretentious about her. She was all frankness, and yet she was mysterious, something one could see clearly but could never fully comprehend. Like the night sky in a poem.

Except, of course, when he couldn't see her at all. Like now. He longed for her, but he could not go to her. She didn't exist, except when she stood in front of him. And wherever she was right now, he certainly didn't exist for her. When he had believed at first that she was a figment of his own mind, he wasn't far wrong. He was also a figment of hers. He wondered if she thought about him nearly as much as he thought about her. Perhaps it was their thoughts that brought them together.

At the moment, all he could think of was Laura.

Even when other ladies were in front of him, vying for his attention, his thoughts strayed to her, as though he could caress her with his mind, and she could feel it. He didn't know what she was, or the meaning of her sudden appearance in his life. All he knew was the way he felt when she was with him, just looking at him with her large, dark eyes.

Understood. Loved. Safe.

And lit on fire, a torch burning from the inside out.

The room was damnably hot. Alaric tugged at his neckcloth—Jeffries tied it so bloody *tight*. And there were too many people about, pressing against him. Ellen had promised him it wouldn't be a crush. He should have listened more closely when she tried to talk to him about the guest list. Alaric felt as though every person he had ever met since the day he was born was in his house. If he listened closely enough, over the din of laughter, clinking crystal, and the strains of music coming from the ballroom, where the string quartet labored to create the appropriate ambience, he might be able to hear the foundation of Stonecross groaning in protest. Waves of heat rose up from the bodies of the guests, whose mingling scents clashed abominably. People always over-scented themselves for a party in an attempt to mask the inevitable odor of sweat that was the result of too many bodies crammed together, dancing and flirting. It was the smell of lust battling with that of propriety. In Alaric's experience, lust usually won out, in one way or another. And then propriety dealt with the aftermath.

Just when he was seriously considering flinging himself from the nearest available window, dinner was announced. Some semblance of the order of precedence was followed. There were few peers present, because Alaric didn't know many, other than some of the lads he went to school with who had come into their titles or retained their courtesy titles while they waited for their elders to pop decorously off into the netherworld. Alaric was glad, not for the first time, that he was not in possession of a title. The Storm fortune had once stunk rather badly of trade, but it was more than respectable now. He was a gentleman with no responsibilities other than to his tenants, and his land steward took care of that. Observing at his social superiors, some of whom were looking distinctly weedy and glad of a gratis meal, despite their pedigrees, Alaric felt a sense of pride in his costly, elegant attire. He used to be quite a young blood, once upon a time. Oddly, he felt rather more interested in his personal appearance than he had in years. It didn't take much probing to realize that it was because of Laura. Because she could shimmer into being again at any moment. He wanted her to be proud to love and be loved by him, even if they could never be together.

As he led Ellen into the dining room, its vast table crammed end to end with laughing, chattering guests, Alaric imagined Laura appearing suddenly among them. What a stir she would create. Especially if she had neglected to get dressed. He hadn't seen her fully dressed since that first day, when he thought he saw her at the front door.

Had she really been there?

He didn't know. He hadn't asked her. He didn't know anything about who she was, or why she was at Stonecross.

The problem was that he had only just begun to think of her as a real person, in the sense that she had lived a life and experienced things he couldn't imagine. Even if he didn't understand who she was, he *had* to stop thinking of her as a creation of his own mind. He couldn't bear the idea that she was little or nothing more.

She was so real. So much more so than anyone who now sat at his table. It wasn't that they weren't fully realized human beings, loveable and interesting, or despicable and petty, in their own ways, just as he was. It was that he didn't know any of them, and they didn't know him. He had never maintained any of his relationships. He had no idea what they were all doing here, pretending to fete him as though he were an old and beloved friend. It was all a beautiful farce, full of blinding footlights and elaborate costumes. Everyone made polite and suitable statements at the prescribed moments, just as they ate their palate-cleansing ices with the correct dainty spoons.

The only palate cleanser Alaric wanted was Laura.

He could taste her now, even as the spoonful of lavender-

and lime-flavored ice melted over his tongue, and Ellen placed a proprietary hand none too discreetly on the sleeve of his coat. He caught sight of the two of them in one of the many sparkling mirrors placed strategically about the room in an attempt to multiply it endlessly, so the light would seem infinite, as would the room, and the number of guests. They looked well together, he had to admit, like a pair of perfectly matched grays about to be bridled to a common yoke, pulling the well-sprung carriage of their union down an endless street. Endless, that was, until one of them dropped dead.

Alaric had to admit that Ellen was everything she should be: beautiful, elegant, her conversation both decorous and entertaining without trespassing upon her partner's wit. She wore the most fashionable garments, and her skin had never spent an instant too long beneath the sun. She would age like a dream, the perfect matriarch for their future brood of show horses. But that was not all he wanted. He wanted much more, and Ellen could never be more than she was, and if Alaric married her, he never would be, either.

Clenching his jaw, Alaric removed his arm from beneath her fingers as subtly as he could, but he saw the flush creep up from her bosom like the blush of pink in the heart of a rose. He used the hand he had taken from her to bring a glass of wine to his lips, so he wouldn't embarrass her. She didn't deserve the impatience he felt. She had every right to expect him to offer for her. He had not behaved like a gentleman. Not strictly speaking. And Ellen was the sort of woman who brought out the gentleman in men who weren't even born to it. That was the problem. With Ellen, Alaric would be obliged to conduct himself with gentlemanly tact in every waking moment for the rest of his life—even, he had absolutely no doubt, in the bedroom.

Whenever he thought of taking her to bed, he imagined her made of cloth beneath her clothes, and stuffed with sawdust, like a doll, her arms and legs, shoulders, neck, and head all made of porcelain. When he laid her back, her eyes clicked shut.

When he thought of Laura, it was another matter entirely.

Which was the very reason why she should be the last thing on his mind as he sat at table with everyone he knew.

His loins tightened painfully beneath the sleek wool of his trousers, and he shifted uncomfortably in his seat, glancing up at the mirror again to see if his lascivious thoughts had bled into his carefully arranged face. Mistaking his sudden movement for a signal, one of the footmen came instantly to his side, proffering a carafe of wine. Alaric nodded, and allowed the man to refill his glass, which he had barely touched.

Just as he had barely spoken to the woman at his side.

Or the man on his other side.

He was a taciturn man, but he knew he was being ridiculous.

He turned to Ellen, who had just finished laughing merrily at the slightly risqué joke told to her by the gentleman on her right. "These . . . centerpieces are very . . . elegant," he said, gesturing slightly to the masses of fruit and flowers festooning the length of the polished table.

She smiled brilliantly, her teeth a row of polished pearls, and he was chagrined by how obviously grateful she was for his attention. He was a bastard. She deserved better. He had known her so long—too long, perhaps—that he often treated her as though she was little more than another piece of furniture decorating his parlor. Even though he didn't want to marry her, he really was rather fond of her, in a nostalgic sort of way.

"You've done a remarkable thing, Ellen," he continued. "I have never seen the old pile looking so festive."

"Only wait until you see it tomorrow," she breathed. "I have some surprises in store for you yet. This is merely the preliminary show."

He smiled as genuinely as he could. "Wonderful."

She returned his smile with true pleasure and lowered her eyes, blushing as though she was a debutante and he her most desirable suitor. He studied her while her gaze was lowered demurely. Did she really feel that way about him? Was he truly the trophy for which she had waited so long, or was he not, by now, a desperate consolation prize? Had he allowed himself to be so blinded that he truly didn't know?

After the ladies rose and withdrew, leaving the gentlemen to their port, Alaric rose and slipped from the room while the footmen were busy with decanters and cut crystal glasses, and the gentlemen were dusting off their bawdier jokes and loosening a few of the buttons on their straining waistcoats. How relieved everyone always seemed to be when left alone with members of their own sex. Alaric didn't particularly enjoy being left alone with anyone, other than his father. He had so few friends. None, really. His truest friends were either dead, scattered to the corners of the kingdom, or shimmering back and forth between nothingness and negligible existence.

He walked silently down the corridor, until he saw a few lady stragglers gossiping on their way to the drawing room.

He ducked into the nearest doorway, and slunk down the back stairs. Inevitably, he nearly ran into a maid on the third story—he was forever running into servants. She was a skinny young thing with bright black eyes and a rather fearsome expression to go with her beak of a nose. She put Alaric in mind of a crow, if there was a corvid equivalent to a scullery girl.

She gave him a penetrating look, the audaciousness of which brought him up short. She didn't drop her eyes, though she graced him with a curtsy, her wilted apron clutched in her chapped fists. "Tara, is it?" he said, examining her oddly handsome little face.

His mouth quirked at the barely concealed mutiny that rose in her expression before it subsided into something slightly more suitable. He didn't enjoy the way her eyes glazed over, as though she was deadening herself. "Tess, sir."

He didn't know why he had stopped to speak to her. It was foolish of him. Servants didn't like to be condescended to. No one did. It was best if they just pretended not to see one another, when at all possible. Jeffries had a marvellous way of acting as though Alaric was an animate mannequin when he bathed and groomed him. He was not given to gossip, any more than Alaric was himself. His entire life seemed to be the thankless pursuit of perfection. Alaric really had no business keeping him shut away at Stonecross, where all he had to do was keep the clothes of a gentleman who never went anywhere or did anything to showcase his precision with a razor and flair with a neckcloth. Poor Jeffries. He would have to give him a pay raise, or let him fly back to London, where his talents could be put to better use.

He nodded at Tess, whose eyes had drifted to the vicinity

of his beautifully polished shoes. "Well, off you go," he said gently.

She gave him a look that sent a terrible chill through him, though he had been sweating through his shirt only moments before in the blazing dining room. It was an expression that reminded him of Laura: too wise and aware, as though all the secrets of existence were laid out before her eyes. As though she could see the whole truth of him, and what was to become of his life. It was not an altogether delightful sensation, and Laura clearly managed to dilute it. This girl hit him with the full force of her unearthly awareness. Why had he never noticed how strange she was before now? She had been just another scrawny kitchen maid, and now she commanded the full force of his attention.

"What is it?" he said sharply, taking hold of her arm. It was as thin as a matchstick in his hand, and he was careful not to squeeze it too hard.

"I've seen her again," she said. "The lady what don't belong."

"Where, Tess?" he asked, tilting her chin so that she had to look at him with her glazed eyes.

"Now," she said insensibly, as though she was in a sort of hypnogogic state. "And then. And always." She blinked blearily, her brow furrowing, her fierce little face gathering into a scowl. "She's in the kitchen, cracking eggs. She's waiting. Waiting for you."

She swooned against him, and Alaric gathered her up, making sure she didn't fall—the girl weighed absolutely nothing. *In the kitchen, cracking eggs. What the devil did* that *mean?*

One of the chambermaids came down the corridor, and Alaric waved her over. "I want you to take her to her room and put her to bed," he told the awestruck girl, who gaped at him with her mouth open. He didn't know her name, and didn't ask for it. "She isn't feeling herself. Can you manage her?"

"Yes, sir," the girl said, dropping a curtsy.

"Never mind that," he told her. "Just take her."

When he was satisfied that the girl wouldn't drop her charge on her head, Alaric left Tess in her care, and strode off, his leg aching slightly after the exertion. The pain told him that a storm was gathering, despite the heat welling up inside the house that made him forget the time of year. As if he could truly forget. October had a way of making itself felt, in every moment.

He ignored it, and charged down the back stairs toward the kitchen.

In his agitation to see if Tess was correct or merely babbling, he nearly didn't notice what had happened.

It was the single most unsettling thing that he had ever witnessed, even given that he had been lately falling rather deeply in love with a specter.

As he descended the final staircase, Stonecross changed.

It wasn't a trick of the light, or the product of an errant shadow. He saw his way very well. And his way was littered with refuse. The plaster was crumbling along the plain whitewashed walls of the servants' stairwell, and the woodwork bulged in the places where unchecked moisture had ruined it. The banister felt like a grossly misshapen limb beneath his hand, and he jerked away from it, wiping his hand reflexively on his waistcoat, as if to rid his skin of its memory. The plain wool runner had disintegrated beneath his feet, and his nostrils were assaulted with the brackish stench of decay. It was as though the house had died around him, and he was standing inside of its moldering corpse.

Heart racing, Alaric crossed the remaining few yards to the doorway of the kitchen. The doors hung loose on their hinges, and when he pressed his shoulder against them, the one on the left shuddered open with a god-awful screech that sent talons of irritation raking along the back of his neck. He glanced wildly about, taking in the wreckage of what had been a very orderly kitchen the last time he had had occasion to visit it. Now, he barely recognized it, with its peeling walls, grime-crusted floor, and broken windowpanes. Only the long plank table in the center was wholly familiar, with his own initials carved on one rickety leg.

Carved when? he asked himself. *A hundred years ago? Two?* The notion sent an arrow of fear ricocheting through his bowels. Was he dead now, wherever he was? And what would happen to him if he couldn't go back? Laura always did. That was true. Even when he didn't want her to. *Always* when he didn't want her to. For the first time, it was a comfort.

In the dimness, he barely saw the figure that darted out of the pantry, cradling something against its chest. Before he could help himself, he let out a yell. The figure froze, staring at him. *Who on earth would be living here?* Alaric moved forward, and picked up a lantern someone had lit and left there unattended. It threw a feeble light over the dimness of the room as he held it up high, barely dispelling the dense shadows. He squinted, and moved closer.

"Who is there?" he said, his voice a low growl in the dimness. There was another flicker of movement, and Laura gasped, dropping what she was holding.

An egg.

It splattered onto the floorboards and over her feet.

Alaric stared at her, stunned. *She's in the kitchen, cracking eggs.*

She pressed her fist to her heart, as if to stuff it back in. "She said you couldn't," she said. "That only I could."

He frowned. "Who said?"

"Tess."

Rivulets of unease trickled down the inside of his collar, but he shrugged them away. Surely he was beyond that. He lowered the light, replacing it on the table before he dropped it, adding his own contribution to the mess on the floor. "She told me you were here. She said you were cracking eggs." He shook his head at the impossibility of what he was saying. "I saw her not a moment ago."

Laura shook her head slowly, with a strange little smile. "No, Alaric. You saw her sixty years ago."

Her words broke over him like powerful waves. He felt like he was drowning in them. He was in Laura's time now. Was it really possible? If it was improbable when *she* did it, now that he was following suit, it seemed utterly unthinkable. He wasn't like her. He was just an ordinary man. It wasn't his place to go traipsing about in time, like a Sunday picnicker in the park.

Alaric reeled drunkenly, flinging a hand out to steady himself on the table. Laura reached out reflexively, as if to catch him, but her hand slid through him. It was almost painful. He could practically feel her fingers slipping through him to the other side of his skin.

"Good God," he said. "So this is what it feels like to be dead."

CHAPTER TEN

"You aren't dead," Laura said, patiently, and then hesitated. "Well, not in so many words."

Alaric frowned at her, his hands cupping the mug of tea she had given him. It was good simply to know what to do with his hands. "I don't understand any of this," he said.

"No one understands it," Laura said, reaching out to touch his hand.

"Where exactly am I?"

"With me." Her voice was gentle. "Isn't that enough?"

He stretched out his fingers beneath her hand, gazing down at the place where she touched him. "I can nearly feel that, you know. I can very nearly feel *you*."

Laura blinked, her smile a slow, sensual caress that sent a thrill through his basest regions. Desire battled with unease as he savored the simple comfort of sitting across a table from her. "Why can I feel you, when I could barely graze your skin before?"

Laura picked up her shoulder, and dropped it. "Because it's just past midnight," she said. "And it's nearly All Hallows Eve."

"Is it midnight?" he said, pricking up his ears to listen. "I didn't hear the clocks chime."

"That's because no one's wound them in many a year," Laura said.

He started up, knocking his knees against the underside of the table. "My guests!" he said, with a self-conscious grimace, though he didn't understand his sudden solicitude. "I've left Ellen to take care of them alone!"

Laura's expression darkened, though she recovered quickly, pressing her hand harder upon his. "Alaric, they've *long* gone home. There is no one here but the two of us."

"What is it?" he asked. "Did I say something to offend you?"

"Ellen," she said softly, gazing solemnly into his eyes. "You *do* have a lady. Are you married to her?"

He cleared his throat, and took a sip of tea. His throat was suddenly dry as the Sahara. "No, not yet."

"But you *want* to marry her."

"Not precisely, no. But I *should* marry her. I should have married her years ago."

Laura nodded, smiling to herself, that same strange little indecipherable smile she wore when telling him how many years had passed in the time it took for him to descend a flight of stairs into the kitchen. "Alaric, that is precisely what you do. And I don't want you to." Her eyes glimmered with tears as she looked at him. "I want you to marry me."

A fierce joy flooded through him, followed by an anvil crashing down, settling somewhere in the region of his bowels. "What do you mean, it's what I do?" he said in a low, dangerous voice. "Why do I have the distinct impression that you understand much more of the situation than I do, much more than you have led me to believe? I thought we were both struggling in the same darkness."

"We are," Laura said. "But I have a torch." She reached into the pocket of the trousers she was wearing. Trousers. He had never seen a woman wearing them before, except in bawdy pictures of sapphists. She was no sapphist, he knew, and though distinctly masculine, the trousers only seemed to heighten her femininity. She could wear a paper bag, for all he cared, and she would still be the loveliest woman he had ever seen.

He watched curiously as Laura pulled out what looked like a trio of playing cards.

She laid the cards one by one on the table, like a gypsy fortune-teller at an autumn fete.

Alaric didn't need to look at them to know they were no ordinary cards. They filled him with a sense of dread. He looked at them, and saw fragments of his own life, the one he was living, and the one to come. The cards knew all. They saw him well. They were a mirror in which he might decipher something other than his face. He didn't want to look. He didn't want to see what Laura saw.

He pushed his chair violently back, and sprang to his feet. "Stop talking in bloody riddles!" he growled, pacing the breadth of the kitchen. He felt the silt of dry leaves giving way beneath his feet. He sensed Stonecross crumbling in on him. Stonecross. His house. The house of his forefathers, as far back as memory.

And now? Whose house was it?

He turned to Laura, who sat watching him. He tried not to dwell on her lips, red as blood, or the thicket of her hair, curling every which way. He ignored the way everything inside of him seemed to magnetize in her direction, like she was his one true polarity.

"If you are real," he said slowly, "and I am here with you, in some other . . . reality, in another time, as you claim, then why is my house in ruins? Why have I no descendants?"

"You died childless," Laura told him quietly.

He nodded, his stomach a knot inside of him, tightening. "And how did you come to be here?"

She smiled briefly. "You wouldn't believe me if I told you."

He stood, staring at her. "I don't think I have a choice but to believe you, so please. Just tell me the bloody truth."

She considered for a moment, as if weighing her thoughts on an invisible scale. "Stonecross Hall is mine. It has always been mine, since before I was born. I've spent my whole life dreaming of it, waiting for it, as it has waited for me. It is my birthright."

Alaric frowned. He had no idea what she was saying. "I don't understand. How is it your birthright?"

She stood then, and crossed to where he stood. She placed her hands on either side of his face, and he could feel the thrumming of her blood, the pulse in her wrists as they cradled his cheeks. "Because you love me, Alaric," she said. "Because you have loved me over and over again, in every moment of time, and always will."

Laura kissed him then, and he felt the full force of her lips on his. Somewhere, he thought he heard a chime sound, but then it faded beneath the rushing of his blood, like a riptide coursing through him. He put his arms around her, and gathered her close. She was not quite solid. There was the sense that part of her was absorbed into him. She gasped, and he was afraid he had hurt her, but she pulled him closer. He picked her up, her feet dangling *en pointe*. He felt her lips graze his jaw, nibbling at the sensitive place below his earlobe. The shock of Laura's body on his, the way he felt as though they were within each other, was the most intimate sensation he had ever experienced in his life. Never had he been closer to anyone. And yet, he wanted more. He wanted to be deeper, closer. He wanted her body to swallow him whole.

"Stonecross is mine because you gave it to me, Alaric," she whispered. "You left it to me in your will, because you knew I would come back to you, again and again. Time isn't what we think it is. It's something so much more. It's infinite. This moment is endless. We will be here like this forever, even after we are both dead and gone."

He pressed her closer, as if to drag her back from that terrible moment. As if he could shield her from death itself.

Then he pulled away from her, and it was painful. He looked searchingly into her deep and glittering eyes. Her lip rouge was little more than a pinkish stain. He had kissed it all away, and could taste it, like sugared roses beneath his tongue. He set her down so that she could sit on the table. He didn't let her go as he sat back down in one of the battered old chairs in front of her. He never wanted to let her go. He clasped his hands around either side of her, still holding her close. Laura held him in the embrace of her thighs, and he pressed his face against her breast, inhaling the scent of her, the thin silk of her blouse cool against his cheek.

"But I *do* die," he said, looking up at her. "Before you are born. I marry . . . another." He needn't name who his wife was to be. "It's already happened."

Laura nodded, a pained expression clouding her face. "It doesn't have to stay that way," she said.

"How can we change it?"

She lowered her gaze. "I don't know." She groped along the tabletop, and brought the trio of cards forth into the light. "But I drew these. They are part of my craft. They know what we cannot. And they tell me it is possible."

She held the cards up one by one. "This card is the Past," she said. "The Lovers reversed. It means that things are not as they should be. That you are with the wrong one. That we are not where we are meant to be, because we are apart."

She held up the second card. "This card is the Present. Fortune's Wheel. It's turning, Alaric. It's always turning, like Time. It isn't static. What has been doesn't need to stay the same. The present can be changed if we let it. If we help it."

She held up the third and final card. "This card is the Future. Death. It doesn't always portend a literal death, especially in the Future spot, because death is the inevitable future of all things. It means *change*. It means the death of all that has been. It means rebirth. And I believe it has to do with us. With the lovers Fate has separated by mistake, spinning forever on the wheel of time, never brave enough to leap off."

"How do you know what they mean?" he asked, scorn edging into his voice. "Or if they mean anything at all. They're nothing more than playing cards. I had a governess when I was a child who liked to pretend at reading such a deck."

Laura shook her head solemnly. "How can you ask me that, after all you have seen? I just . . . know. The cards tell me.

I don't choose them randomly; the cards choose the reader. It's not a parlor trick, Alaric. Remember the mirror? A lot of girls play that game. But how many of them do you suppose actually summon their future lovers?"

Her voice was hypnotic. Alaric felt drawn ever deeper under her thrall. He wanted to believe what she was saying was true. He wanted nothing more than to clasp her hand and leap with her into the unknowable void, no matter if they landed on their feet somewhere, or simply drifted forever in the blackness.

As if reading his thoughts, Laura clasped his hands in hers. He felt a surge pass between them, and the room, which had been growing . . . thin, somehow, started to shift back to where it belonged. The Stonecross in which Alaric lived was pushing back through, like an arm sliding into a sleeve, the hand slipping out at the other end. And then he was back, in Laura's time. His Stonecross had receded. Alaric's flesh shivered and the hair on his head stood up. He felt stronger. He felt solid. He felt as though she was anchoring him to her world.

"Alaric, do you trust me?" Laura gazed deep into his eyes, her expression solemn.

"Yes," he said, with no hesitation.

"I know we haven't been able to control moving in and out of time—well, before now, you couldn't even do it—but I think if we do it together, we can go into either world. Did you see the way the room flickered, and then came back when we touched? It's trying to take you away from me, but I didn't let it. Now I want you to let it take you—and try to bring me with you."

"I will try. Though I have no idea how to do as you ask."

"Think of Stonecross," she said. "*Your* Stonecross."

Alaric did as she instructed. A cool sheen of sweat had broken out on his brow, and Laura, too, gleamed in the lamplight. He could smell her, a fresh surge of her unique scent wafting from the folds of her clothing. He closed his eyes as she did, and concentrated, holding her hands. He thought of the way the library smelled like leather and dust, and old, dead cigars. He thought of the feel of the carpet in his room beneath his feet, the room that was Laura's now. Because he had given it to her. Because he wanted everything that was his to be hers.

He felt a peculiar lurch in his insides, as though he was in a carriage that had come to a too abrupt stop. He felt thrown sideways. It was the most terrifying sensation of his life. He felt as though he was being suspended in a void of utter and complete nothingness, without a body to house him. Was this what it was like for Laura when she came to him, or was it different for someone gifted like she was in the arts of the uncanny? He didn't know. All he knew was that he felt like he was dying, and that there would be absolutely nothing to catch him when he finally fell into the abyss.

And then something righted him again. Alaric's body came back to him, a sudden rush of molecules. The relief was so palpable, it registered as pain. He felt Laura's arms about him, and he swayed, grasping onto her as though he was drowning, and she was the only handhold he could find. Thank God—he was alive! He was not about to be sucked away. He wanted, in that moment, nothing so much as to live. And never to experience such a tearing away, body from soul, again.

"It's alright, love," she said, stroking his face lightly. "Open your eyes." And he did, blinking as she came into view, her large brown eyes filled with emotion. He pulled her close, clinging to her as he gazed around.

They were standing together in the warm kitchen, *his* warm kitchen. He recognized it, though he hadn't spent time there since he was a boy, pestering the cook for a sweet. Though redolent of all the leftover dishes from dinner, it still retained its own particular smell, as familiar to him as the scent of his own skin. Houses were no different than people. They were singular. He would know the smell of his home the way he would know the smell of Laura's perfume: instantly, and with some part of him that he couldn't name. He looked about in relief at the amazing restoration of the most humble room in his home. A kettle was singing discordantly, and the stove glowed dully with banking coals. The pots hung where they should, their bright copper bellies gleaming as if in greeting.

Behind him, he heard a startled cry.

They weren't alone. One of the scullery maids who had been busy scrubbing up the last of the pots and pans and miscellaneous crockery dropped a platter when she saw them. She didn't look alarmed beyond a commonplace startling, and so she must not have actually seen them appear as if from nothing.

"Beg pardon sir, madam," she said, with a curtsy. "I didn't see you there. You just come out of nowheres, like a pair o' ghosts!"

Laura pressed a hand to her lips, stifling a laugh, and the girl gave her a funny look out of the corner of her eye, taking in her outlandish garb and cropped hair.

Alaric drew himself up with as much restrained hauteur as he could muster, given the fact that he was holding the hand of a lady while in a state of dishevelment—and in the kitchens, no less. But he couldn't maintain it. Instead, he threw his head back and laughed like he hadn't laughed since he was a child and propriety hadn't yet got hold of him.

It was absurd and wonderful to be alive, to be holding this woman by the hand. Even time itself couldn't keep them apart. There had never been lovers like them since the history of love began.

Still holding Laura's hand, he bowed gallantly to the baffled maid, and pulled his lover away.

"**W**on't they wonder where you've gone?" Laura asked breathlessly, as they sneaked their way along the corridors, ducking occasionally into a deserted room to avoid stray houseguests who had gone to use the lavatory, or to keep an assignation of their own. Laura would have liked to have a better look at them, but Alaric pulled her impatiently along. He hadn't let go of her hand for a single moment since they had crossed the invisible border between their worlds, and Laura didn't complain. Though she felt more solid, more anchored in Alaric's Stonecross than she ever had before, she wasn't altogether certain what would happen if he let her go, and she didn't want to find out.

She heard sounds of laughter and music wafting up from the rooms below. "I thought the party wasn't until tomorrow night," she said.

"It isn't. Not the main event, at any rate." Alaric pushed

the final door at the end of a long corridor open, and peeked cautiously in before pulling Laura in with him. "And these are not even all of the expected guests. My sister has yet to arrive, for instance. Lizzie is always late. For everything. Even," he said, with a smile that was half exasperation and half adoration, "her own wedding. She kept us all waiting at the church for over an hour while she had her hair redressed."

"You have a sister?" Laura asked softly.

Alaric nodded. "This is her bedchamber," he said. "One of the few unoccupied at the moment. We keep it for her, for when she comes. She likes to sleep in her old bed when she is away from her own."

Laura gazed about, taking in the rich furnishings and polished furniture. She had seen the room in a wholly different state: musty, filled with dust and rotted silk, the windowpanes broken and the plaster crumbled over everything. Now it was as lovely as a dream, all rose-colored satin and lovely little landscape paintings. A fire was laid in the grate, and Alaric, letting go of her hand without thinking, bent to light it.

Laura's heart lurched, expecting no doubt to be torn back to her own time, as she had so many times before.

But no such thing happened. She didn't so much as fluctuate. She was as real here as she was in 1926. *Perhaps more so*, she thought. *Because he is here . . .* That was it, wasn't it? He was her anchor. If Laura could just hold on to him, she could stay. And perhaps, they could help each other go back and forth. Could they? She didn't know. But it would be a grand adventure to try it out. Laura didn't much care which time she landed in, as long as he was there with her. For now, she was where she wanted to be—and when. She would hold on to Alaric, and he would pin her in place like a butterfly behind glass.

She watched him as he oversaw the fire, lighting a spill to carry the flame to the sconces that housed fresh tapers. The warm light spilled across the room, dispelling the deepest shadows, unravelling the copper strands that streaked Alaric's mane of hair. She hadn't known many men who didn't shear their hair nearly to the scalp in the back, though in her time they wore whips of longer hair in the front, slicked back with brilliantine.

She found there was something so . . . primal about the sight of an impeccably dressed gentleman who wore his hair thick and long. It was as though he knew he was, deep down, little more than a barely civilized animal who might at any moment forget his manners.

Laura could only hope.

He rose from his knees, though she rather liked the sight of him there, and turned to look at her, his eyes full of a fire that was no reflection. Heat flooded her at the sight of his slightly wilted shirt, the buttons gleaming in the candlelight, begging to be undone. His frock coat seemed to billow about him like the raiment of a king. He stood regarding her, his eyes sliding over her body. She wore a new blouse—such a thin, transparent thing—silk the same color as her skin. It would tear so easily in his hands. She could tell he liked the way her breasts strained at the yoke, the collar unbuttoned far enough that if she bent over, she would expose nearly every inch of her bosom. She longed to take his hands and place them over the wild drum of her heartbeat. She wanted to wrap her legs around him and breathe every breath he took as if it was her own.

She could see by the way his eyes flickered over her, and how his hands moved restlessly at his sides, that he felt the same way. Alaric's chest rose and fell. His throat pulsed above the sedate collar with its dark cravat. He looked like the hero of a nineteenth-century novel, tortured by passion and filled with pent-up longing for things he could never ask of a lady.

He wanted her. She could almost taste how much.

She was damned glad she wasn't a lady.

"Alaric," she said, in a low, husky voice hardly her own. "Don't you think it's time you undressed me?"

CHAPTER ELEVEN

He crossed to her so quickly, it was almost as though time had folded them together again. She was suddenly enveloped in arms that gathered her up as if she weighed as much as a wisp of smoke. She was a sturdy woman, despite her willowy limbs, unused to feeling delicate around the men of her time, who had needed so much more from her than demure womanliness. Here was a man who needed her in a way no one ever had. She could feel his need, pushing against her as they kissed. His hands pressed and kneaded her hips, fondling her buttocks through the seat of her trousers. He unfastened them with a solemnity Laura found endearing, his eyes soft with wonder as they dropped to the floor. His hands slid up her sides beneath the watered silk of her blouse. Her nipples tightened deliciously as his thumbs stroked them through her camisole. She could feel a gathering sweetness low down in her body, culminating beneath the tangle of curls that shielded her sex. She was wet. She had never been so wet. She wanted him to touch her, to find the place inside of her that only another person could reach and that, despite her experience, no one ever had. There was more than one first when it came to love.

Alaric unbuttoned her blouse with a tenderness that brought an unnameable emotion to the surface of her heart. She could feel it washing through her, a searing tide of desire and vulnerability. She was not even undressed yet, and already she felt fully naked before this man, who had until only a few days before been a stranger.

"Don't stop," she told him.

"I'm not stopping," he murmured. "I just don't want to miss any part of you."

She sighed, and smiled as he slid the camisole up over her upraised arms, flinging it aside so that it, too, was only a small crumpled thing on the floor.

Alaric gazed at her in wonder, though she was still far from naked.

"What is that . . . item you are wearing?" he said, awestruck. "It is most strange. And . . . wonderful. There is so little of it. Just like everything else you wear, it barely covers you."

Laura laughed. She ran her hands over the garment in question. "This," she told him, "is a brassiere."

His eyes widened appreciatively as he reached out to stroke the filmy lace. "And those drawers," he breathed. "They, too, are positively miniscule."

Laura looked down at herself, admiring the curves of her bare thighs and trim calves. She sashayed a bit, turning a little pirouette so that he might take in the full effect of her modern underpinnings. "Do you like them?" she asked, laughing as he grabbed for her. "I don't suppose ladies of your acquaintance would ever dare wear such scandalous things, though in my time, some women don't bother wearing undergarments at all."

"How wonderful," he murmured, running his hands over her bared back, raking his fingernails lightly over her shoulders and up the length of her neck. He cupped the back of her head in his hands, tilting her neck so he could nuzzle her throat. "I love your hair. I love your lips. I love everything about your body."

Laura melted to liquid in his arms, her roving hands making their own inventory of his anatomy, which was rather difficult in his fully dressed state. When her brassiere came away in his hands, and her drawers slithered to the floor, and she was utterly naked, she pressed him back against the bed before he could gather her closer, forcing him to lounge back as she stood between his knees. Alaric stared at her dazedly, swallowing hard as he took in every bare inch of her. He slid his hands over her hips, grazing the gentle convex of her belly as his fingers went to the place that ached most deeply for his touch, but she pushed them away.

"Not yet," she said huskily. "First it's my turn to see what you've been hiding under all of that beautifully starched linen."

He groaned impatiently, but complied, his hands roaming over only the more demure parts of her exposed flesh—flank, abdomen, the full undersides of her breasts. It was a torture almost too exquisite to be borne, one she once thought she would only ever be able to imagine. And yet, it was only the beginning of what she hoped he might do to her before the night was through. Tiny incendiaries of anticipation exploded along the length of her spine. She trembled as she touched his face, her thumbs tracing the lush contours of his lips, the bold curve of his nose and jut of his jaw. He closed his eyes, and pulled her hand to his lips, suckling each finger in turn, the inside of his mouth a silken cavern she longed to fill with various parts of her, one by one, until he had had his fill.

If she didn't see him naked in the next few moments, she would go mad.

Laura pushed his immaculately brushed dinner coat from his shoulders, tossing it aside. She unbuttoned his waistcoat dexterously, after which she reached to unfasten his trousers, pulling a snowy expanse of crumpled linen from his waistband to reveal an abdomen taut and rippling. It occurred to her that he was going to be much more complicated to undress than she had been, and the thought of all the layers of gentlemanly attire that lay between her body and his sent a deepening tremor of impatience through her. She took hold of his shirtfront, and simply tore it open. An explosion of buttons cascaded across the bedspread, and more than one seam rent in two.

"Oh dear," she said, eyes widening. "Terribly sorry. I've never known my own strength."

Alaric contemplated her with something close to astonishment, though it looked much more like delight. The golden sheen of his chest and abdomen exposed, candlelight licked his skin as Laura longed to do. Her eyes raked over him with a hunger she didn't bother disguising, and she did what she wanted, running her mouth over his flesh as though branding him finally as her own. No other woman could ever possess him as she did.

She licked the faded hatchwork of battle scars that filigreed his flesh, from the most delicate to the cruelest. Beneath her roving tongue, Alaric shivered, the places where he had been wounded more sensitive than the flesh surrounding them. In his skin, Laura tasted not only the salt of his sweat, but the texture of his whole history. Flashes of his experiences came to her as she grazed on his skin. She saw things both beautiful and unspeakable, and swallowed them all, as though drinking in a part of his soul. Whatever happened to them, wherever they went, and no matter if they could never make love to each other again, Laura could play back the jumbled scenes of Alaric's life on the insides of her eyelids long after the imprint of her body on his had faded into memory.

Sliding her breasts along his torso, she followed the concave between his pectorals to the hollow of his throat. She caught his mouth in a ravenous kiss, devouring his lips as though they contained some essential nutrient she must have, or die. Then she stopped suddenly, and pulled back to look at him. "I'm not a virgin," she said, as if to explain her obvious familiarity with the body of a man. "Just so you know. Don't expect some coquettish miss who you must mollycoddle and convince to let you ravish her. I'm a woman, with a woman's desires."

"Thank God," he said, exhaling, a slow smile crinkling the corners of his delicious mouth. His amber eyes were gleaming in the half dark like polished pennies. "I don't want to have to be a gentleman."

"Please don't be," she said.

Taking her at her word, Alaric dragged her against him, the astonishing impact of her skin on his sending a jolt of electricity through his body. It was like being struck by lightning. Suddenly he felt the room shift around him, and they were neither in his world, hers, or the next. He flipped her on her back, and the rigid sleekness of his erection grazed her thigh as he parted her legs to touch her. The veil of his hair slid along her skin, and her nipples ruched into tight little buds as his tongue fondled each of them in turn before trailing lower. He spread the folds of her sex as though peeling an exotic fruit. He devoured her with the same hunger and rapt attention he would apply to a sun-ripened fruit.

"You taste like a peach," he murmured, as her juice ran down his chin. Her fingers twined in his hair, her thighs quivering as she gasped, shuddering with pleasure.

When she came, he could feel her climax as if it was his own, and when he thrust into her, it was a collision of cosmic proportions, like an asteroid colliding with the atmosphere of Earth and burning away. He could feel the reverberations of the pleasure he had given her drawing him in, and it took everything he had to hold back. Laura gasped at the fullness as she took him in, wrapping her legs around him and drawing him deep. She rocked her hips as he thrust into her with powerful strokes, their bodies moving together with piston-like intensity and precision.

She felt like oiled satin. Her breath tasted of cloves. The scent of her skin drove him wild. He could not go deep enough. He couldn't be close enough. There was no such thing.

Her hair tumbled over her face, and her mouth was a kiss-stung oval of delight. Alaric could feel the delightful jiggle of her breasts against him as he surged ever closer to his own crest of pleasure.

Pushing him over, Laura urged him wordlessly to shift places with her, so she could straddle him in the dominant position. He had never experienced a woman moving on top of him, and he nearly spent himself at the sight of her riding his eager cock, her straining thighs and jutting breasts sleek with perspiration. He gathered them in the cups of his hands, tweaking and rubbing her pretty nipples. She arched her back, thrusting her hips in such a way that Alaric could actually watch his shaft sliding in and out of the glistening wetness that held him. He fondled her, pressing his thumb against her hidden pearl until she slowly climaxed again. He followed swiftly in her wake, the waves of pleasure tearing through him like wildfire. He murmured hoarsely every oath and every prayer he knew, until words gave way to the guttural cry that was the first holy utterance.

Laura collapsed on top of him with a weak moan that he sucked from her lips as he withdrew and coiled himself around her, face to face, his arm cradled along her spine. They were both slick-skinned, drenched in the only substance that quenched what it had ignited.

"One doesn't learn *that* in finishing school," he murmured appreciatively into her ear, when he could speak. She giggled, hiding her face in his shoulder.

"I suppose you think me utterly wanton?" she said. "Isn't that a word you use these days, to describe women like me?"

"There are no women like you," he said, tucking a damp curl behind her ear.

"Not here," she agreed, snuggling against him.

"Not anywhere," he said.

Laura smiled, and pressed her lips to his chest. He ran his fingernails slowly up and down her back, and she nearly purred. He loved the way their skin stuck together, as though they were truly fusing into one person. His eyes grew heavy, and he blinked, afraid that if he fell asleep, she would simply disappear. He didn't know the rules. He didn't know if there were any. They seemed to be making them up as they went along.

"In this time," he said, "are you truly not yet born?"

"Not for years and years, yet."

"Then how is it you can exist, here and now with me?"

She looked up at him, her neck arched against the pillow. "I really don't know, Alaric. I only know that I do, and that I have never felt more alive than when I'm with you."

"If you . . . stayed, here, with me, what would happen when you *are* born?"

Laura rolled onto her back, her leg still hooked around him, and her body pressed alongside his. She cradled her head on her arm, the sinuous curve of her underarm upraised. Tiny beads of perspiration pearled her collarbone, a necklace of her own making. "I don't know. But my time isn't a good one, Alaric. It's a dangerous time, when the whole world has been at war with itself. I've seen things I can't erase from my mind. People have done things that take away their humanity, and now they are expected to carry on like decent citizens."

"I know what war is," Alaric said.

"Not war like this," Laura said quietly. "We can never be the same, any of us. Being here with you makes me feel like none of that could ever happen."

"Maybe it won't," he said gently, running his palm over her sweet flesh.

"Oh, it will," she said. "And then it will happen again. Time isn't the only endless cycle."

They were quiet together then. In the distance, Alaric heard a low rumble of thunder, though no rainfall accompanied the sound—it was a dry storm he had felt in the air, and it was finally beginning to break. In counterpoint, the last strains of music from the gathering below drifted up to settle like a tender blanket on their skin. The guests would soon retire for the night, no doubt wondering to where their host had disappeared. He had a reputation for this sort of behavior, and he knew no one would be unduly alarmed. Ellen would smooth everything over. She always did.

"Poor Ellen," Alaric murmured.

Laura stiffened slightly. And then relaxed. "Yes," she agreed. "You must tell her . . . something, Alaric. This can't go on."

And as if summoned by the sound of her name, the door swung open, and Ellen herself stood in the doorway, her voluminous silhouette standing out in stark relief against the lamp-lit hall behind her. She held a taper high, sending forward a billow of light that illuminated the lovers in their nest of tangled sheets and twined limbs. Alaric threw his arm across Laura's chest, as though to shield more than her nakedness. Ellen stared at them with an unreadable expression, her mouth working soundlessly. Laura and Alaric stared back

"I have been searching all over the house for you, Alaric," she said finally, a shrill quaver creeping into her voice. "Do you care to explain yourself?"

Ellen turned to look at Laura, who scrambled up against the headboard, the bedclothes pulled up over her breasts, her eyes dark with conflicting emotions. Everything in her shrank back from this woman who had barged her way in on the most intimate moment of Laura's life as though it belonged to her, instead. "And you," Ellen said. "I don't know who you are, but I think you should know that this man is, for all intents and purposes, engaged to me."

Laura's mouth opened, but no words came. There was absolutely nothing she could say. She felt as though her heart had been removed from her body to be served to this woman on a plate, like in a gruesome folktale. There was a raw emptiness, a gaping hole. The overbearing assurance of Ellen in her silk gown and elaborate ostrich feathers seemed to sap every ounce of courage from her body. Alaric didn't belong to her. He could never belong to her. Not once she left this bed.

She turned to look at him, her face on fire. "Alaric?" she said hoarsely, the word seeming to come from some other person, far away.

"That isn't true," Alaric said in a low voice. He laced his fingers with Laura's and gave them a reassuring squeeze, though her hand was quite limp. "And you know it, Ellen."

"It is true now," Ellen said, a steely calm coming into her voice. She came fully into the room, and shut the door behind her. She set the candle on the bedside table, and sat down in the delicate little chair that adorned the corner of the room as though she had every right to enter whatever room in Stonecross she liked. Which perhaps she had. In this time, anyway.

Her spine was as straight as a poker, righteous indignation lending her complexion the flaming color normally reserved for desire. Laura thought her rather lovely, but there was something missing. There was nothing inside of the carapace that made her seem a delightful lady to all who looked upon her. Laura could see that she was nothing but a lovely, stuffed sawdust doll with eyes of glass and cold, porcelain arms. Arms that had more right to hold Alaric inside of them than Laura had.

She felt a tremor of fear wash over her. Women like Ellen were powerful. A lady like that had power simply by birthright that Laura would never know, or want to. It was the power of societal position, and of entitlement. She could not compete with it.

Laura had never felt so humiliated in her life. If only Stonecross would open up and swallow her back to her own time. But Alaric was gripping her fiercely, and it was impossible to push him away while she could still hold on to him for even a few moments more.

"Do you really think I would give you up to some trollop? Did you set this up to be rid of me?" Ellen laughed, her eyes skimming with distaste over the state of the bedroom, their clothes strewn about, and their huddled, naked skin. She seemed to take delight in the way she held them hostage. For as long as she liked to sit there, looking at them, they couldn't rise and dress. She had them at a distinct disadvantage, which gave her obvious pleasure. "Alaric, take all the trollops you like to your bed, as long as you are discreet and don't humiliate me in public. Well, any more than you already have over the past ten years. An engagement announcement at the party tomorrow should take care of that part nicely."

"Ellen, I am not going to marry you," Alaric said with a steady voice. "I love Laura. I'm going to marry her. You are right, however. I owe you more apology than is possible to convey. I truly am sorry. I should not have allowed this farce to go on as long as it has. I think we both knew that it was no good, only neither of us would admit it. You should have gone and married long ago, and you still can. Any single gentleman you encounter is yours for the taking."

Gesturing dismissively as if all the single gentlemen in the kingdom were of no consequence, Ellen shook her head scornfully. "Do you truly believe you can just marry this . . . this chit, and all will be well? Do you think your friends will accept her after I have told what I have seen to all who will listen? No one in polite society will have ought to do with her. She will be shunned in every drawing room and assembly house from Plymouth to London." She angled her head to stare coldly at Laura, who had not moved during the entire exchange. "Who are you, girl?" she asked imperiously. "Who is your family, and what fortune have you, to set your cap so high? It is a fool's errand, to spread your legs to catch a husband. If it were not, I would have tried it myself years ago."

Finally, Laura found her voice. "My love for Alaric isn't a trap," she said, her heart hammering as she levelled her gaze. She would *not* let this woman see that she was distraught. "I don't want to own him, or force him into anything. I only want to love him. If I thought you felt the same way, I might feel bad for taking him away from you. But you don't, do you? He is simply a pretty plaything to add to your box of trinkets."

Ellen stared at her haughtily, appalled by her audacity. And then smirked, shaking her head. "*His* love is the trap,

you little fool—not for him, but for you. Can't you feel it closing around you? Escape while you still can, and pray you don't
have a whelp in your belly to pay you back for your folly."

Laura looked at her, all of her anger deflating. She felt
nothing but pity for this foolish woman who thought love was
nothing more than a sparring match. She had stood before
this woman's grave. She had seen her pitiful epitaph. It was
far different to speak to a living woman over whose remains
one has stood and whose future one knows than to commune
with a lingering spirit. Ellen, though a living woman, filled
Laura with a revulsion she never felt for Alaric when she had
thought him a ghost.

"You poor thing," she said, without thinking. "You have
no idea why your life is so empty."

"I don't require a lesson from a little slut like you on the
subject," Ellen spat, coloring. If she had been standing closer,
Laura had no doubt she would have been dealt a swift slap
across the cheek with one of Ellen's pretty white hands. She
could see the way her fingers convulsed into a fist before lady-
like grace got the better of them.

"Ellen," Alaric said, his voice flooding with barely controlled fury. "Do not insult the woman I love. I will marry her,
and you will leave this house as soon as it can be arranged. I
am sorry for the wrongs I have done you, but malice won't
win back the years we have wasted. It's time for us each to live
our lives. Can't you see that? And I will live mine with Laura."

Ellen scowled, her pretty face crumpling like that of a
child who has had its best toy taken away. "You won't!" she
said, stamping her lovely slippered foot. "No one will accept
her. And a gentleman may not break an engagement with a

lady. Everyone knows we were meant to be man and wife, and that you all but offered for me before you left for that bloody war of yours. You *will* marry me, Alaric Storm. Or I will ruin both of you."

Alaric's mouth dropped open. "You would really hold a man who doesn't want you to the childish declarations of a boy who was about to have his head blown off on another continent, just to save face?"

Her face grew solemn. "Yes, I would. In the end, our faces are all we have." And then, a pious smile twisted her small bud of a mouth. "And what do you think your father would say, Alaric, if you threw me over for this harlot of yours? It would kill him. You know it would. Just as you know he has always wanted me for his daughter-in-law. You know that was always his intention. If you do not agree, I will go to him right now, and tell him everything I have seen, and everything you have said to me. And he will make you do what you know is right."

Rising triumphantly from her seat, having just dealt her trump card, Ellen looked as priggish and smug as any woman ever had who knew she had a man by a very delicate handhold. "I will leave you now to reconsider your position, and to rid yourself of this . . . woman. When you have quite come to your senses, Alaric, you needn't say a word about this matter. We will pretend as though nothing has happened. Our little secret—like a bond to seal our marriage."

She swept from the room, taking her candle with her, the door shutting so quietly behind her, it seemed like the whole altercation was merely a mirage.

Thunderstruck, Alaric turned to Laura. He looked into

her eyes, taking her shoulders into his hands so that she was forced to face him. She turned her face away. If she looked at him now, it would kill her to do what she knew she must. "Don't listen to her," he said, in a voice so low Laura could barely hear it. "I love you. I will spend my life with you."

"Even if I can never be anything more than a ghost, Alaric?" she said softly. "We don't know if we can even stay in the same era together, except at this time of year. I know I seemed so certain last night, but dawn is coming. And nothing seems very possible in the cold light of morning." She lifted her hand. It quavered in the slowly breaking light. She was turning into a shaft of light herself, dimming and shimmering. "Look at me. It's taking all my concentration just to stay in this bed with you. If you let go of me, I will simply disappear."

He gripped her still tighter, his fingers digging deeper into her shoulders. "But tonight," he said urgently. "Surely tonight will be different. It's All Hallows. If we can just find a way to keep you here."

"And then what?" Laura said, trying to hold back her tears while her heart quietly broke. "You heard what Ellen said. I will bring you nothing but disgrace. Eventually you will hate me for it."

"No. Never. We can go away. We can start a new life, somewhere else."

"And your father?"

Alaric said nothing. He set his mouth in a line. "I'm not going to let you go."

Laura smiled, leaned forward, and kissed him more deeply than she ever had. Their lips melted into a single mouth, and for that last moment, they were inseparable.

"You have no choice," Laura said, breaking away. "I love you, Alaric. Good-bye."

She closed her eyes then, and though Alaric dragged her against him, shaking her as though trying to rouse her from the dead, she shimmered for a moment, and was gone.

CHAPTER TWELVE

L aura opened her eyes to her own Stonecross, the tableau of peeling paper and falling plaster seeming ugly to her for the first time. She had willed herself to emerge in her own bed, rather than in the bed in which she and Alaric had been lovers. She preferred this bed, because it belonged to Alaric. Three decades after his death, it was still his. Everything was. Stonecross itself would only ever belong to Alaric in her mind. It was redolent of him. He permeated every crumbling inch of plaster, each yard of rotted silk that hung in beckoning tatters from bedposts and window frames. Laura was one small fragment in the midst of it all, and she, too, would always belong to Alaric.

She curled into a small ball in the great bed, drawing the musty bedclothes over her nakedness. She had left her clothing behind, crumpled on the carpet like shreds of discarded skin. The only thing he would ever have of her, unless those paltry textiles had disappeared with her, as they no doubt must have. The thought brought hot tears welling up in her eyes, and she squeezed them shut, letting the salted water fall. It felt good to cry. She never cried. Now she would cry enough to last her the rest of her life, and then she would stop. She didn't think there would be much worth weeping over after this. She would be dry as a rain cistern in a time of drought. Nothing would grow in her heart. She could feel it shrinking in, curling on itself and pressing everything so tight it could do nothing but suffocate the things it held inside it.

After a long, sodden interval, Laura sat up and wiped the tears away, scrubbing her swollen face with her hands. She ignored the way she could still smell Alaric, smell the salted perfume of sweat and sex that clung to the creases of her fingers. There would be other lovers. They would help erase the imprint his body left on hers. Laura would launder her body as if her skin was a stained sheet. Each time she took a man to bed who wasn't Alaric, there would be less and less trace of him left. She would scrub herself raw with the flesh of other men until she was again a nameless, anonymous woman who had sex for any reason but love.

She would go back to London, and become that woman again as soon as possible. The flat in Piccadilly was still waiting for her, as were her midnight companions in the dance hall below. She would be along again with the cat, who was at that moment snuggled at the foot of the bed, his belly upturned. She could hear him purring. She would have to ride into the village after she packed, and arrange for a car to come collect her and take her to the station. There was a train at midday, thank God. If she had to wait any longer, she would have hired the car to take her all the way to London. Either that, or walk, carrying the cat's basket as he yowled all the way. Laura would do whatever she had to do to make sure she never laid eyes on Stonecross again.

She got up, shivering in the heatless room. She had left the fire behind with Alaric, and Stonecross was as frigid as a sepulcher in the chilly dawn. The cat stretched, unperturbed in his fur coat as Laura struggled into several layers of clothing. She wore trousers again, and her brother's old sweater that had begun to unravel even more. She didn't bother glancing into the mirror, or taming the riotous curls that stood out all over her head. She needed to get to the village as fast as possible. If she didn't leave Stonecross that morning, she might never leave it at all.

She certainly didn't want to.

And that was dangerous.

She couldn't risk ruining Alaric's chance at living a normal life without her popping in on him every time the moon phase was auspicious, or the days darkened toward an Equinox, or All Hallows came back round again. She was a bloody fool to listen to Tess, who really didn't know what she was talking about, any more than Laura herself knew what she was doing. It was like feeling her way in the dark, with occasional bursts of lightning that allowed her to see for moments in time the mess she was in. It was no way to live. It was no way for Alaric to live. She would end the cycle right here and now.

But could she really stop it? The fact that she found herself in Stonecross again, with everything exactly as she had left it, clearly meant that nothing had changed. She was more than a little surprised to wind up back in the house. She thought she would end up . . . where, exactly? She didn't know. She had changed things in the past. Things had changed. Surely that should mean that the present was different, too. She just didn't know how it was different. And how much different she could make it, so that it would stop happening.

The idea that Alaric had still willed his house to her after everything that happened was more than a possibility; he had to have done so, or else she would be back in her flat, trawling for shillings in the palms of people's hands, never the wiser. She shoved the evidence of Alaric's continued devotion to the back of her mind. It changed nothing. She could never go back to him, and she couldn't stay at Stonecross, where the temptation might be too great. And the memories of the time she had spent in his arms would haunt her as surely as any specter. She preferred ghosts she could dispel. That was how she would treat herself, for Alaric's sake, like a haunting that could be banished back to where it belonged.

Laura went from the room, turning back to the cat. "I'll be back for you," she told him. "Mind you don't go wandering off, or I swear I'll leave you behind to fend for yourself."

The cat yawned, unconcerned, and went promptly back to sleep.

Laura sped along the road to Cropton, and she really meant to go straight there. But when the mist blew away from the cemetery, clinging to the leaning monuments like a winding shroud, she was compelled to stop. It was All Hallows, after all. She couldn't ignore the dead man she loved. She would visit him one last time, in the only place where she could do him no harm.

She flung the bicycle down among the crumbling tombstones, and followed the fingers of mist where they pointed. The many-chambered vault of the Storm family was as she had left it: row upon row of patriarchs, tier upon tier of their lesser relations. It was gloomy in the dawn light, and Laura wished she had thought to bring an electric torch with her to light her way. She wasn't afraid. She just wanted to be able to see the place in which she would leave Alaric behind forever.

The scattered weeds she had left the day before clung in wilted clumps to the surface of the polished stone crypt, and Laura's hand trembled as she brushed them away. She couldn't read the epitaph—the light was still too dim to illuminate even such bold lettering.

While she waited for the day to brighten, Laura wandered over to the wall of lesser crypts, though she didn't much want to honor Ellen's grave, even on this day. She couldn't feel much sorrow for the bones of the woman whose claim on Alaric vanquished her own. Laura had loved him for a few nights. Ellen had been married to him for decades. They still had no children, or at least no sons. But Ellen had Alaric, and no doubt he had learned to feel something for the woman who commanded his honor as a gentleman.

Laura steeled herself as she approached her rival's grave.

And then frowned, peering into the gloom.

There was nothing there. The compartments were empty.

Alaric's tomb stood alone in the vault, his bones unaccompanied in their final resting place.

He hadn't married Ellen Wright after all. He couldn't have. Unless she had managed to live far past her allotted three score and ten—but then, she would be living in Stonecross herself.

Laura's heart leapt painfully as she whirled about to face the stone carapace that held the remains of the man to whom she had made love sixty years before. A shaft of light gathered strength as it wafted in through the stained glass window nearby, sending shards of colored light dancing across the epigraph. Laura leaned close, barely able now to make out the words.

ALARIC STORM III
BELOVED SON
VETERAN OF THE CRIMEA
31 OCTOBER 1835 –16 MAY 1891
HE WAITS FOR LAURA
IN HEAVEN

Seeing her name inscribed in cold marble was like a punch in the heart. Laura had never felt such pain. It was excruciating. Alaric hadn't married Ellen, though she had done everything she could to blackmail him into it. He had waited for Laura, and she never came. She had just left him there, to pick up the pieces. To wait, in a state of steadily decreasing hope, through all the long years that were for her nothing more than a moment. A step from one room to the next over an invisible threshold.

She thought she was being honorable. She thought she was saving him from a life of resentment and public scorn as the man who married the floozy he had taken to his bed. She thought his marriage to Ellen would save him in ways she never could. Instead, she had condemned him to a life of loneliness and pain. And even so, he had *still* left her his house, his fortune, in the hope that she would change her mind, that the waiting would stop.

Laura's own waiting had only just begun. She would know intimately the torture he had undergone, for love of her. Because she would go through it herself.

Unless she had the courage to change her fate, and his.

Her spirits lifted at the thought. Could she? Was it possible? Could she really go to him forever that night, or was it only ever to be a yearly visitation, when the worlds were close, life and death overlapping enough to grant them passage? Would they grow old together that way, like but unlike any other couple? Would there be children? Laura's mind whirred as she fled the crypt without a glance backward. She didn't know what would happen. She didn't understand any of it. But she had to go back. Alaric had never given up on her. He had spent his life waiting. She owed him something far more than she had given him.

She leapt onto the rickety bicycle and flew back to Stonecross as fast as she could pedal. The wind tore at her, and the eerie moorland reached toward her on all sides, as if claiming her as its own. She was mad to think she could stay at Stonecross. She had been even madder to think she could leave.

Peddling blindly, she nearly ran the old woman down as she crested the final rise. Tess was standing out in the road, in front of the lane that led to her small croft, her skinny legs stuffed like matchsticks into her requisite pair of battered old wellies. She looked like some sort of Bog Woman straight out of an Irish myth, bent on portending a sign of great evil.

"I saw you go by when I was out for my morning walk," she said, eyeing Laura as the bicycle skidded to a stop, nearly toppling her over her handlebars.

"I didn't see you," Laura said. "And anyway, I wouldn't have stopped."

"You didn't do it," the old woman said reproachfully, ignoring Laura's pointed comment. "You didn't stay with him. He waited for you until the moment he died."

"I know," Laura said.

"You saw the inscription, then?" Tess nodded with satisfaction. "I chose it myself, after the master passed away and I was left to take care of the funeral arrangements. I was the housekeeper by then, and he trusted me with such matters. I knew it would pique your interest. Mayhap it changed your mind."

"I didn't have a choice. Ellen would have ruined him. And if she didn't, I would have."

"You did ruin him," Tess said. "You're ruining him still. It ain't too late. It's never too late. If you don't do what you ought now, mayhap you'll do it next time. Or the next."

"I'm not listening to you," Laura retorted. "I should never have listened to you."

"And yet, here you are, peddling as mad as you can back home to Stonecross," Tess cackled. "You know you got nowhere else to be."

Laura scowled. "That's my business. What I want to know is how you seem to know everything. Wherever I see you, whenever I find you, you know everything that has happened or might happen or will happen. How is that possible? You shouldn't remember me. Everything keeps changing so much that every time you see me should be the first."

Tess tapped her temple the way other people tapped their noses, in a knowing, smug sort of way. "It's my gift.

I see things all at once, layered together like cheesecloth. Time is so thin this time of year, I can see straight through, in every direction. Even when it changes, I still know what's happened. And I can tell you, missy, I don't much like the way it's gone."

Laura sighed, deflating, all of her obstinacy melting away. "Neither do I. And I'm not sure what I can do about it, if anything. No matter what I do, I'm going to have to leave him. It takes more concentration than I have just to stay with him for more than ten minutes, and I have to cling on to him the whole time like he's a life preserver in an endless sea."

"And you are the same for him," Tess said mulishly. "If you cling on long enough, you'll find the shore. Now, get on home. And do your best, young woman. I'll help you if I can."

Laura frowned. "How?"

Tess waved her gnarled hand, and turned away back up the lane. "Just ask me, when it's time."

Laura stared after her for a moment, and then got back on her bicycle. She rode home, looking for all the world like some kind of woman knight on a quest for something holy, her hair blowing back in the wind, her brother's ratty sweater her only armor against the fray.

The house was waiting for her, as it had been from the moment she was born. The lichen-encrusted stone cross leaned like a wanderer in the wind, as though lurching toward her with its arms outstretched. Laura felt a strange compulsion to wrap her own arms around it, but she managed to turn away and make her way up the drive. She mounted the crumbling steps, and threw open the door, which sagged on its hinges as if exhausted with all of her coming and going.

Laura walked back in, surveying her moldering kingdom. All the while she had been half waiting for a glimpse of Miss Havisham in the shadows, and now she may well become her. It was a better life than any she could think of outside of Stonecross.

She skated across the layer of leaves and dust that coated the once-gleaming marble floor, and came to stand before the one object in Stonecross she had avoided examining: the great marble figure swathed in rotten white sheets. Laura was drawn to it as if to a touchstone, and she obeyed her instinct. She didn't remember it being present in Alaric's day. At least, not the part of his time that she had shared with him. Clearly, it had been erected sometime later, in the interim years between when she had abandoned him and when he had gone to wait for her in some less earthly realm. The thought of him still existing somewhere, watching over her and waiting for the day when she would inevitably join him was oddly comforting. She had never really thought of her own dead that way, though she often urged other people to do so, in order to lessen the burden of their grief. Now that she was one of her own bereaved patients, she too needed to believe what she was telling herself, in case she never saw Alaric again.

Her hand trembling, Laura reached out to touch the cold flesh of the statue's exposed ankle. The plinth on which it stood was breast-level, and she could very easily catch hold of the billowing tatters of cotton that obscured it from her gaze. It looked so much like a stiffened corpse stood on its feet that Laura shivered. It was the things that people made, more than the ghosts that lingered behind them, that frightened Laura. Steeling herself, she tore the sheeting away. It came down with a horrible tearing sound, a rotted cocoon in her arms that she quickly flung away. She stood and looked up at what emerged, still pale and shining after standing in protected layers for so many years.

It was of a woman, standing with arm upraised to cradle her head against her own shoulder, a cropped tangle of curls partially obscuring one of her eyes while the other looked boldly out. It didn't have the dead look Laura normally attributed to statues of its kind. Not that there had ever been anything like it. It was a statue like no other she had seen of nineteenth-century provenance. Though it had elements of Art Nouveau aesthetic, it was much more modern—the lines cleaner, the composition spare and very Art Deco—with distinct elements of the Grecian.

The dress was simple. A scrap of silk the color of skin. One strap slid down the pale arm, exposing the breast, which was a breathtaking replica of a breast she knew very well. The thighs beneath were delightfully curved and seemed supple, despite the immoveable material from which they had been carved. Laura slid her hand from one dainty foot over the ankle and up the back of the slender calf. It would have been very daring. As daring as Laura herself.

For it *was* Laura. She looked up the towering length of the statue and into her own smiling face. That smile she wore only for Alaric. The smile he must have wanted to remember for the rest of his life.

She knew then what she should have known the night before, when Alaric tried to make her stay. Nothing she was, nothing she would ever be, could make him ashamed to call her his wife. Not even if she could only be his wife for a few hours on one night of the year and spend the rest of it as a ghost in his hallway. There were worse ways to live, and Alaric had already lived them. It was time to try for something more.

She went up the stairs two at a time, and burst back into her room. Their room. The room she would share with Alaric even when they couldn't be in it together. The cat sprang up and took off, sorely offended at the abruptness of her entrance. Laura stooped to dig under the bed, where she had stored her luggage, and dragged out a valise. She opened it, and began tossing her clothing about. What did one wear to a nineteenth-century birthday party? Especially when one had barely been born when the nineteenth century ended. Everything she owned was scandalous.

But then, that was one of the things Alaric loved best about her.

She chose a gown, a terribly costly one she had bought frivolously, knowing she had nowhere she could wear it. She draped the shining, shimmering thing over the back of the dressing table chair, and admired it. It was a thing of perfect beauty. When she saw it in the shop window, she simply had to have it. After the purgatory of sensible dresses and cheap gowns she had worn since the war, she longed for the cool, slippery kiss of silk sliding over her skin as she moved.

She took out her cosmetics and hairpins, arranging them on the surface of the vanity in orderly rows like battalions of toy soldiers. They did not call it a beauty regimen for nothing; Laura would need all of her troops assembled. She was going into the most important battle zone of her life. She went down to the kitchen to boil water for her bath, already imagining the warm caress of water that would carry all the fear and insecurity away, banishing the quivering leaf Laura had been and leaving only a perfumed, svelte vamp in her place, rouged, powdered and dressed to kill. Or, more accurately, to resurrect.

CHAPTER THIRTEEN

"I don't understand what the matter is with you tonight, Alaric," Lizzie said, batting him none too gently with her fan. "I've never seen so many people turn up simply to watch a man they rarely see blow out the candles on a cake."

"It was all Ellen's doing," he said gruffly, downing yet another glass of champagne. He grimaced. The damned stuff was watered, as if they were all a pack of giddy debutantes. No doubt Ellen was trying to wean him before the wedding she still seemed to believe would take place. "You know how she loves a spectacle."

Lizzie tilted her head quizzically. "Is everything alright between you?" she said, lowering her voice. "She gave me to understand that there was to be a very interesting announcement tonight."

"Only if she forces me to announce in front of everyone she has ever known that I would rather marry one of the scullery maids than tie myself to her for the rest of my life."

Lizzie's mouth fell open, and she grabbed her brother's arm, dragging him to the edge of the room where the crowd was thinnest. "You don't mean that. All this dillydallying, and then you mean to jilt the poor girl? It's scandalous, Alaric. I didn't think you had that sort of meanness in you."

"I never offered for her," Alaric said mutinously, tossing his glass on the heavily laden tray of a passing footman. He glanced at his sister's bewildered face, and sighed, his shoulders deflating. "Though it's true, I have behaved very wrongly. I should have sent her away years ago. I just didn't . . . care very much, one way or the other. I thought if I ignored the situation long enough, she would get exasperated with me and go of her own accord. I didn't want to be unkind. But she never did, and I realize now that I was being very unkind to her indeed. Though you must believe that was never my intention."

"So you have never bedded the girl?" Lizzie queried seriously. "All of Society thinks you have, you know."

"God, no!" Alaric said, more loudly than he meant to. "I would never do such a thing. And even if I would, she wouldn't."

Lizzie lifted a pale blond eyebrow. "Do not be so sure of that, brother. She may seem innocent, but our dear Ellen is a calculating bit of muslin." She tapped her nose knowingly. "Women sense these things about each other, much more so than men do. That being said, Ellen would make an excellent wife, Alaric. I've always thought so. She would be able to . . . to . . ."

His sister colored uncharacteristically, and Alaric laughed deprecatingly. "Manage me beautifully, the way I cannot seem to manage myself?"

Lizzie lifted her chin. "Precisely," she said crisply. "You know you need it."

"What I need is to take hold of myself," Alaric told her. "An entirely different method to achieve the same end, which I agree is sorely overdue."

Lizzie smiled, clearly relieved. "Why, what brought this on?"

Alaric said nothing for a moment, and then told the truth. "Love."

Lizzie's eyes widened, a bloom of gleeful anticipation creeping over her face. "Why, Alaric! You sly thing! Who is she?"

Alaric sighed, and shook his head. "No one you will ever know," he said. "I cannot be with her. But she has changed my life for the better. From now on, I will actually live it, instead of moping about, drinking, and waiting for it all to be over."

Lizzie frowned, and opened her mouth to say something, but instead gazed about inquiringly as a rush of murmuring seemed to sweep through the crowd.

Alaric scanned the room half-interestedly. He saw nothing but the crush of people in their wilting finery, the dazzle of diamonds round the ladies' damp throats as they whirled in the arms of their partners, and the bobbing plumes of ostrich feathers as the ladies who weren't dancing gossiped behind their rapidly whirring fans. The glower of jack-o'-lanterns amid swathes of harvest-inspired decorations on the punch table and the glare of fully lit chandeliers drew his eye momentarily. Everything was as Ellen arranged it. Nothing was amiss. What could possibly have fascinated everyone so much that they had all stopped guzzling champagne, dancing, and gossiping? It was as if the clockwork that controlled their bodies had wound down at once. Even the bloody string quartet had come to a standstill, the musicians in their fine black coats gaping like schoolboys staring into a sweetshop window.

Alaric frowned. What the devil was going on?

And then, suddenly, he saw her—Laura, standing across the room, just inside the doorway.

His whole body flooded with relief. Alaric had never felt so glad to see another person in his life. He was so overwhelmed with joy that he nearly laughed out loud, hysterically. Like an exhausted child on its birthday, Alaric was helpless with emotion. All he could do was gaze at her hungrily at her as she made her way through the crush.

The other guests seemed to give way before her without realizing it. They gaped at her, as he did, but for different reasons. To their eyes, she looked fantastical, so . . . out of place. She was dressed in a red gown of diaphanous silk that barely clung to her shoulders and didn't even try to hide her knees. She glimmered all over with glass beads sewn into a wild pattern on her dress, and her shorn hair was sleek and complexly waved, tucked behind one ear. Her lips were coated lavishly in Laura's signature blood-hued lip-rouge, and she smiled softly, looking all around her, as though she couldn't quite believe what she saw.

Laura walked in a way Alaric had never before seen a woman walk who wasn't naked—a slinky strut, like a panther. He realized that it had something to do with the fact that she wasn't trussed within a whalebone cage, the way the rest of the women were. She wore no voluminous layers of petticoats and drawers. She was naked beneath her clothing. She was utterly free, and yet she had allowed herself to

become his. She had dared to do what Alaric had never allowed himself to dream: she had come for him.

If she was aware that she was causing a sensation by appearing nearly naked in front of a crowd of Devonshire's finest
families, Laura didn't let it show. She smiled and nodded to
the people who stared at her and murmured volubly as she
wove her way through the crowd, which parted before her as
though making way for royalty. For that is what she seemed
to Alaric: a queen in red, graceful and sensual, in complete
command of every inch of her body. Perhaps that was how
all women were in the future. If so, it was a damned wonderful improvement on the current model. Alaric felt a trickle
of shame creep up from his stomach. He knew it was largely,
if not completely, due to male conventions and control that
women were the way they were. They were caged literally—
in tightly laced corsetry—and they were caged in spirit. He
himself had been keeping a woman in a cage for over a decade,
a woman he didn't even want. All of his anger and sense of
righteous indignation toward Ellen melted away. Alaric
aimed it toward himself, where it belonged.

And then, he pushed the guilt away. He could think of
nothing but Laura.

He opened his arms, and in front of everyone who thought
they knew him best, he gathered the half-naked woman into
his arms. The gasp was audible. Not only that, it was tactile.
Their collective shock and disapproval washed over him in a
wave, and he let it. Laura held him steady. He was safe in her
arms.

Her gaze swept downward, and he saw the shimmer of
cosmetic dust clinging to the creases of her eyelids. They

looked like the wings of a moth, fluttering. He wanted to kiss them, and every part of her face, from brow to the tip of her chin. In the distance, he heard a clock chime midnight. His lover had never felt more solid in his embrace. He pulled her close, inhaling the maddening elixir of her perfume as if breathing in her very essence. "Dance with me," he whispered.

She nodded, and Alaric raised his hand to signal for music. The dance floor emptied as the scandalized guests made way for the pair, their chatter very nearly swallowing the delicate strains of the waltz. The customary twinge of pain Alaric always felt when engaged in such exertions seemed to fade completely, and he danced as he did before the war had ruined him. For the first time in his life, he realized that a thing could be *unruined*, if only the correct analgesic was applied.

"Laura," he said simply, gazing down into her flushed face. "That was the bravest thing I have ever seen. And I love you for it, even more than I loved you before. Thank you."

She smiled, her adorably crooked teeth gleaming like a row of imperfect pearls. "I was wrong to leave you like that last night," she breathed. "Or rather, sixty years ago. Or . . . whenever it was. I was afraid." She squeezed him, pulling him closer. "Not for myself. For you. For the mess I had made of your life."

"Clearly, it was a mess I wanted," he said. "After all, I left Stonecross for you. I had planned to visit my solicitor on Monday, to change my will. Did I do it?"

"You did. And it was still there when I got back."

"And then what happened? What made you change your mind?"

She shook her head. "I'll tell you all about it sometime. All you need to know is that it was love. I love you, and it made me come back."

"I know the feeling," Alaric said. He scooped her up, and danced her about, her feet dangling as he drew her lips into a deep kiss. "Let's dance all night," he murmured between breaths. "Whatever happens, hold onto me until . . ."

"Until I go."

"Yes."

And she did. They clung to each other like the sole survivors of a shipwreck. The room receded, and there was nothing but the two of them swirling about on an eddy of music, weightless, timeless, eternal. Their eyes never left each other's. Their arms were an unbroken lock holding each other fast. They were one person. They were one soul.

Until Ellen stormed into the room, eyes blazing, her face breaking like a clap of thunder. She grabbed Alaric by the arm, nearly colliding with the pair as she dragged them to a stop.

"What do you think you are doing?" she hissed. "I thought this little tart of yours was gone for good, or at least hiding in one of the unused wings. I never thought you would actually bring her as a guest to the party I gave for you! How could you humiliate me like this after everything to which we agreed last night?"

Alaric frowned, pulling Laura closer, one arm around her holding her snugly against his side. She wrapped her own arm about his waist and held him tight, squeezing him with reassuring strength. "*We* agreed to nothing, Ellen," he said in a low voice. "You threatened us, and thought it would be enough to force me to go through with this farce of a marriage. You were wrong."

Ellen stared at them, furious, unable to speak. And then her face crumbled like that of a disappointed child. Alaric reached out reflexively, and stroked her cheek like a fond and baffled relative. "I'm sorry, Ellen," he said, with genuine remorse. "I've treated you very badly, and you've always done your best to be good to me. You will make some man a fine wife, I've no doubt whatsoever. It just won't be me."

Ellen's face cleared rapidly, though vestiges of a cold fury still remained. She nodded, threw back her shoulders, and reared her hand back to slap Alaric full in the face. The audible *crack* of her kidskin-covered palm reverberated through the room. Alaric's head snapped back, and he touched his cheek in amazed silence.

"If you think I will sully myself in a marriage alliance with you, Alaric Storm," Ellen said shrilly, tossing her head for dramatic effect, "you have quite mistaken me. I will be leaving in the morning. Do not attempt to follow or prevent me."

The room erupted into a fresh din, and Alaric threw back his head and laughed as the entire mob surged forward to get a look at Ellen as she exited the ballroom in high dudgeon. "Lizzie was quite right," he said, pulling Laura from the molten center of the crush. "That girl will land on her feet well enough. No doubt she will make a brilliant match before the Season even begins. And my name will be mud from here to Grosvenor Square."

"Do you mind very much?" Laura asked seriously, as they slipped out onto the terrace.

"I could not possibly care less," he said. "Now that I have you."

Laura's face was troubled as she gazed out over the water. "Yes, but for how long? And how much will you care once I have gone?" She lifted her hand to gaze at the volatile solidity she enjoyed. "I am only here because All Hallows makes it possible."

"How do we know that, for certain?" Alaric said, turning her back round to face him. "It's only speculation, really. We know we made more possible last night than we thought we could. I came through to your side, when you thought I wasn't able to. And you stayed with me until it was almost daylight, when before, you faded almost as quickly as you appeared. I couldn't even touch you."

"Tess said . . ." Laura mused abstractly. "Well, she didn't say anything really helpful, as a matter of fact. That woman is very keen on the cryptic. She simply said that the veils between worlds are thinnest this time of year, and that tonight they disappear. She was also in rather a lather to have me come here to be with you forever."

"So it must mean that it is possible for you to do so, mustn't it?"

Laura shrugged helplessly. "I had hoped so. But if I stay, how will we live? Everyone thinks I'm mad, and a harlot! No one will have anything to do with you after this."

Alaric shrugged, unconcerned. "We will go away. Live abroad."

"Where I will grow my hair out into a more womanly style, put on a corset and a bustle, and live like a submissive little Society matron?" Laura said, shaking her head. "No. I can't, Alaric. Surely you must see that. I must be free. And if we were to have children, their grandchildren would only be caught up in the same war I barely escaped. I won't have it. I just won't."

Alaric sighed, nodding. He gathered her up against him, and kissed her curls. They were sleek and oiled in a very strange way, and smelled of some kind of hair tonic. "You do have the oddest hair," he murmured.

She smirked, and nuzzled closer to him. His long hair tickled her face. "So do you."

"Laura?" he said, after a moment. "What on earth is a bustle?"

"There you are," an exasperated voice trilled from behind them. Laura and Alaric jumped in alarm, turning about defensively to come face to face with Lizzie.

Alaric sighed in relief. "Lizzie, you startled the bloody hell out of me," he growled. "You always were terrible for sneaking up on a fellow."

"And *you* were always doing things you shouldn't, forcing me to sneak about in an attempt at catching you out." The woman with the bright, curious eyes inclined her head less than subtly in Laura's direction. "Case in point."

Laura flushed, and bit her lip, allowing Alaric to shield her with his arm. Alaric blushed himself, but then drew himself up. "Lizzie, this is Laura. The woman I love. She is . . . foreign. Laura, this is my baby sister, Lizzie."

Laura reached out to grasp the other woman's hand. "I am pleased to meet you," she said, doing her best to look and sound like she was from somewhere far away—which wasn't at all difficult.

Lizzie shook her hand enthusiastically, surveying Laura's person with frank fascination. "Where exactly are you from, my dear? That is quite an . . . unusual—and daring—frock you're wearing. I like it!"

Laura laughed, and smoothed her hand over the shining silk. "Thank you," she said. "I . . . I was given to understand that it was a . . . fancy dress ball. This is what I wear when I want to feel like I am someone else, for an evening." Which was true enough.

"I wish I had your nerve," Lizzie said admiringly.

"Lizzie," Alaric said, bringing them all back to the point at hand. "I don't want you to be alarmed if I have to . . . go away for a while. Perhaps a long while."

Laura threw him a penetrating look, but said nothing.

Lizzie gazed back and forth between them. She nodded briskly. "I understand. Or rather, I understand as much as I want and need to."

Alaric smiled, and pulled her close. Laura backed away to stand at the balcony, alone. Alaric hugged his sister fiercely. "Whatever happens," he said, "if, for some reason, I can't come home, I want you to promise me you will look after Father."

Lizzie blinked, surprised. "Of course I will, Alaric. You needn't even ask."

Alaric nodded, reaching out to take his sister's gloved hand. "I know that, Lizzie. Thank you. You've always been a good sister to me. As for Stonecross, it will be Freddy's, of course. The will remains as it was."

"He would rather have his uncle," Lizzie said, emotion finally flooding her voice. She *hated* to cry. She said it spoiled her looks, which were only as much as she could make of them. Eyes red from weeping never helped anyone.

"I know," he said gently. "But I love Laura. I need to be with her. She is my one chance, Lizzie. Before I met her, I wasn't living. I was simply existing."

Lizzie nodded tightly, dabbing her eyes with a gloved finger. She patted Alaric fondly, stood on her toes to kiss him, and then crossed over to where Laura was pretending, with very little success, to be invisible. Lizzie surprised her by pulling her into a fierce embrace. "Be good to him," she said, "Or I will want to know why. And leave me the name of your *modiste*."

Laura laughed, and nodded. "I will. On both counts. Though she may not have what you want available for quite some time."

Lizzie waved her hand as if it was of little consequence. "I have time. The Season doesn't begin for *ages*."

Alaric and Laura exchanged amused glances. Lizzie gave them a final wave, blew several kisses, and then left them alone.

Laura snaked her arms about Alaric's waist, tilting her face back to be kissed. "We may not have much time," she told him seriously.

"And we may have all the time in the world."

"Either way, my love, what do you wish to be doing while we wait for the sun to come up?"

Alaric laughed, and smiled wickedly. He held out his hand. Laura took it, and they slipped back into the house and up the servants' stairs to the bedroom that, in every possible era, was theirs. Their clothes came away, and they fell naked into the bed.

They made love.

They made every kind they could imagine. And they never let go for a single moment.

Later, when they had exhausted themselves, Laura lay in Alaric's arms. "It's far beyond midnight," she commented, raking her fingernails over the taut flesh of his abdomen.

"Mmmm," he murmured appreciatively.

"And I'm still here with you, as I was last night."

Alaric nodded sleepily. "Yes. I can feel you."

"But I don't think I can stay," she said in a small voice. "Not forever. Look at my hand." She lifted it up before his face, and the watery light of the gibbous moon shone right through it.

Alaric grabbed it, and kissed it fervently, nipping at the tip of her thumb. "Can you feel that?"

"Yes. But it's fading," Laura said sadly. She struggled to sit up, and Alaric did the same. They held hands, sitting cross-legged like naked children depicted in a color plate inside a book of fairy stories. Laura grew paler while he watched helplessly.

"Take me with you," he said.

"I can't," she said. "If I take you, your father will be alone. I haven't even met him yet, but I cannot take his son from him. He needs you, Alaric. Especially now that Ellen will be leaving."

Alaric didn't argue. He knew it was true. Though there was Lizzie, she was not precisely the nurturing sort. He had always taken care of everything at home, as he should. She had agreed to bear the burden for Freddy until the lad came of age. Was it too much to ask of her? Uncertainty fluttered inside of him for a moment before biting decisively down.

"And you can't just leave your family, your estate," Laura said, as if reading his thoughts. "Your life is here, at Stonecross."

"I want my life to be with you," he argued. He felt the way she was sliding away from him in a way that had nothing to do with the physical. If he wasn't careful, she would slip between his fingers like sand in an hourglass.

"Perhaps next year," Laura said gently. "After you've had time to think, and to arrange things. And I can always appear to you, as I have. Perhaps not with the same solidity, but I can come to you, I know it. And then, next All Hallows, maybe . . ."

"Anything could happen between now and then," he said mutinously.

"I wish Tess was here," Laura said. "She could tell us. She sees all possible futures. It's her gift."

"Not yours?"

Laura shook her head. "No. I only see the dead." And then she lifted her head, her mind whirring. "But Tess said something else, yesterday morning, when she found out I didn't stay with you. She said, *Just ask me, when the time comes.*"

Alaric's brow furrowed. "What do you think she meant?"

Laura lifted her hand. She could see Alaric through it, shimmering as if on the other side of a pane of antique glass. "I don't know, but I think now would be a good time to ask her."

Alaric leapt up from the bed, and flung his dressing gown at Laura as he hunted about for some clothing of his own. "Put this on," he said. "Now. I'll take you to her."

CHAPTER FOURTEEN

When they finally found her in her room at the top of the house, after scandalizing several other virtuous young maids by their state of *dishabille*, the young girl who was Tess in Alaric's time was sitting up stock-straight in her bed, her arms cradled about her flannel-clad knees. She scowled at the pair of them in a way that made her look very much like her future self, the wizened country crone of Laura's time.

"*There* you are, at last!" she chided, climbing out of bed. "If you wasn't along in one more minute, I'd of gone and fetched you myself, no matter what you was doing."

Laura gaped at her, bemused. "How did you know we needed you?" she asked.

"I told myself, of course!" she said, shaking her head irritably, as if it was the stupidest question she had ever heard. "I come over strange, like I was having a fit or something, same as when I saw you in the kitchen last night. It was mighty queer seeing the house like that, all come to pieces. I'd of thought someone would take care of it better, but that's none of my business." She gestured to the small desk in the corner, where several sheets of foolscap lay scattered, blotchy with ink and scrawled all over in a childish hand. "I was doing a bit of trance writing, and I got a message from myself from your time." She nodded at Laura. "And just in time, too. Or I wouldn't have knowed what you was talking about when you come to see me."

"I didn't know you could write, Tess," Alaric said, before he could stop himself.

"I can't," she said, with infinite patience. "Not yet, anyway. But *she* can. The old lady me. And she read what she wrote to me, too, inside my brain, like."

"We don't have time for this," Laura said, in a strangled voice. "Not if we don't want to wait until next year to have this fascinating conversation. I'm about to fade away completely. It's taking everything I have just to keep hold."

Tess nodded brusquely, all business, and held out her hands, one to each of them. "Take hold of me, and squeeze tight," she said. "The old lady me said I was like a sort of . . . rudder, steering you where you've got to go. On account of me being from both of your times."

Laura and Alaric exchanged glances, and seized the girl by her scrawny hands, which were surprisingly strong. Laura felt a jolt of power surge through her, and she felt as solid as she ever had, even in her own time.

The room began to flicker between the tidy, spare little nest it was now, and the hollow, frigid cell it was in Laura's time. It was as if a child was standing in the doorway, flashing the light on and off—only it was *time* that changed, back and forth. And then it seemed as though more time periods joined in, and a series of different rooms flickered through, like a magic lantern show spun out of control. Laura felt a little sick, her hand slipping in the slick sweat on Alaric's palm. She clasped it tighter, looking into his face, anchoring him to her. She knew it was harder for him than it was for her.

"Hold on," Tess said calmly, and she herself began to change, from the scrawny waif she was now, to a series of fierce young women, to a middle-aged woman with the same dark brows and beaky nose—until she was the old woman Laura knew well. "Don't stop here," she told them. "This is no place for you, either. Laura's life can't stay the same—that's the missing element, I warrant. You must both sacrifice in equal measure the worlds you have known."

And then, as though she hadn't been standing there, holding on to them, Tess disappeared altogether. There was nothing where she had been. Not even a shadow, or a faint glimmering. Tess was gone, and Alaric and Laura were standing alone together in the room she had occupied. It was now a simple storage closet with whitewashed walls and a scrubbed wooden floor covered in stacks of cartons and a few sheet-covered oddments of furniture.

"Where are we?" Alaric asked, dazed.

"I think the better question is *when*," Laura said, gazing around.

"I suppose we had better find out."

They crept cautiously out into the narrow corridor, and followed their usual route back down to the main floor using the servants' stairs. The plainly decorated corridors gave no hint as to the possible passage or indeed reversion of time, but Laura and Alaric each opened a few of the rooms along the way, attempting to make an evaluation. Some of the rooms looked very similar to the ones Alaric knew well, but the draperies were different, and the walls papered with patterns he didn't recognize. Some of the rooms had items in them of which only Laura understood the use, things like radio cabinets and gramophones. She pulled Alaric away, before he became too astonished to move.

There were objects she didn't recognize, either. Strange rectangles that looked like picture frames, except there were no pictures, only a terrible opaqueness, a blank blackness that she didn't like. She felt like they were watching her, willing her to fall into the void at their centers. She closed the doors to the rooms that contained them quickly.

The main foyer was unchanged. The marble floor gleamed, and the place where the two sides of the great staircases met and formed an enclave was empty. No marble version of Laura stared down at them. But all around them were the faces of Alaric's family, serene and reserved in their gilt frames, and perhaps a little friendlier to look upon. Laura felt somehow that they were glad to see her, and even gladder to see their wayward son.

"There are more of them," Alaric said, awestruck. "Many more."

He was right. The portraits extended past the one in which Alaric himself resided, his penetrating gaze still managing to send shivers of awareness through Laura's softest places, though the real man stood beside her, his arm around her holding her close and safe.

"Excuse me," a voice said, behind him, "I don't know if you know this, but the house is closed the day after Halloween. Only, we've got to clean up the grounds a bit. Firecrackers and jack-o'-lanterns. That sort of thing. You can come back tomorrow, though, during regular hours."

Laura and Alaric turned slowly around to find a very familiar-looking young woman contemplating them with tolerant amusement. Her dark hair and fierce brows were not quite as prominent, nor was her nose. But she looked very much like someone they knew.

"Regular hours?" Laura said faintly.

The girl nodded apologetically. "I wouldn't mind myself, but I don't, like, make the rules. The National Trust runs this place. I only work here."

"I see," Alaric said carefully. "And what about the family?"

"Oh, they don't own it anymore. Gave it to the British people in 2006. It's a Grade One listed building," she said proudly. "They visit sometimes, and some of them still live in the area."

"Have you worked here long?" Alaric asked. "You look very familiar."

"So do you," the girl told him, giving him a look of frank admiration. "You a cousin or something? Of the family, I mean."

He smiled. "Yes, something like that."

"And yeah, I've been here awhile, since I was sixteen. My great-great-great-gran, or someone, used to be a maid here. So it's a family tradition, I guess."

Laura smiled wide. "That's wonderful, to have you looking after the place. I'm sure the house feels like it has a friend."

The girl grinned. "Yeah, the old pile and I get along famously." She looked them over again. "You folks just getting in from a Halloween party? You look like you're in fancy dress." She raised her eyebrow at Laura's choice of attire. "You know, sort of."

"That's right," Laura said. "We had a bit of a knees-up, to tell you the truth, and thought it would be a lark to wander in here and see what the quality were up to. Terribly sorry if we've been a nuisance."

"It's no prob," the girl said, "Really. It gets pretty boring in here when the house is closed. Nobody to talk to. You can browse around a bit, if you want to, but if you see anybody but me coming, you'd better leg it. I don't want you getting trouble."

Alaric smiled, and bowed elegantly. "Thank you, Miss . . ."

The girl blushed and giggled, waving him away. "It's Tess. Tess Jones."

Laura and Alaric stared, and laughed as if hearing the punch line to a particularly delightful joke. "Lovely name," Laura said in answer to the girl's raised eyebrow. "We've been thinking of naming our firstborn Tess, should we have a girl."

"Cool. Anything else I can do for you folks?"

"Yes," Laura said, "As a matter of fact, there is. You said it's the day after Halloween. My friend and I must have drunk more than we realized last night, because for the moment, I can't seem to remember the year. Does that ever happen to you? I don't know how a person can forget that, but . . ."

Tess laughed, and sighed, rolling her eyes. "I forget my own name sometimes, when I've been drinking," she confided. "So I'm not judging anybody. It's November first, 2012."

Alaric's arm tightened to a vice around Laura's shoulder, and she had to grit her teeth into a smile to keep from crying out, in both pain and shock. "Thank you," she said faintly. "I don't know what I was thinking."

"Sure," Tess said. "You have a lovely day, now. And try not to get lost on your way home."

"Too late for that," Alaric said tightly as they waved and smiled, ducking out the door. "What the bloody hell are we going to do now? If we throttle her great-great-great-granddaughter, do you think Tess will feel it, and come to our rescue?"

Laura laughed. She took his hand and pulled him along. It was a beautiful day. The air was crisp, and she was only wearing a pair of dancing shoes, but she felt wonderful. She felt like she was free to breathe, free to live, for the first time. She didn't know what world they were in, but she was sure it was the world they were meant for, because they were finally in it together.

And then her stomach lurched, and her eyes widened in sudden anxiety. "Alaric! Your father!" she cried, pressing her hand against his chest. "You left him behind after all, and it's all my fault."

He shook his head, drawing her against him. A thrill of delight went through Laura as he held her without worrying that she would disappear. Somehow, she knew those days were behind them.

"Don't worry about Father. Lizzie will take care of him, and Freddy will take care of Lizzie, and on and on until now. You and I will take care of each other. That is how it was always meant to be."

Her eyes widened again. "Oh, God! I forgot the bloody cat!"

Alaric laughed. "Tess will take care of him. And if she doesn't, cats are canny creatures. I'm sure he can take care of himself."

"Oh, well, it can't be helped, either way. A cat is more than a good trade for you."

"I should hope so, my dear," he said, with dignity, gathering her to him. "Though I am not nearly so good at catching mice, I am excellent company in bed."

Laura smiled, her whole face lighting up from within. Leaning dazedly against her lover as they lingered in the driveway, Laura gazed about her. "I don't know where we are, Alaric," she said dreamily. "Or when. But I think we're going to love it here."

She kissed him then. Her lips were warm and sweet on his. Her hands in his hair sent shivers down his spine. They kissed for a long while, standing in front of the house that had brought them together, over and over again. And though they might never see Stonecross Hall again, they would dream of it, for the rest of time.

ACKNOWLEDGMENTS

I would like to thank:

My husband Neil for all of the love and support you've lavished on me over the years, not to mention all of the love notes scribbled on the backs of grocery store receipts and midnight trysts and the drive-in theater.

My mum Roxanne for all the unflagging devotion as my constant reader, and the well-stocked bookshelf she has always kept for me to raid. And thank you to my mum's wonderful husband Gord, for all of your kindness and enthusiasm over even the most meager of my successes.

My dad Kelly, who shared my fascination with ghosts so much that he decided to become one. I hope the Elysian Fields are wondrous, and that you can read this book from there . . .

My delightful in-laws for never batting an eyelash at my impractical career choice! I hope to make you proud.

My wonderful editor Chelsey Emmelhainz for taking a chance on a complicated love story that transcends both time and, at times, logic. You are clever and brave!

Everyone at Avon Books who helped bring this book to life, from the copyeditor to the cover designer and publicity team, and everyone I haven't mentioned whose jobs I don't have a clue about.

My dearest friend Shivanee, for all of the small-hour assignations we keep together while the rest of the world dreams.

My oldest friend Sarah for all of the *Star Trek* fan fic we wrote together back in the day, and the many hours spent acting out all of the nuances of our imaginary worlds.

I'd like to shout a thank-you across the pond to my dear correspondent Miss Mariana Heron, whose epic replies to novel-length letters sustain me in my belief that gossiping about things that happened several hundred–plus years in the past is *not* irrelevant.

Last but not least, thank You, whoever you are, holding this book. I hope you like it, and that after you're done with it, you'll pass it on to someone else so they can enjoy it, too!

MORGAN KELLY writes historical romance thanks to an obsession with nineteenth-century Gothic novels that has plagued her (in a good way) since childhood, when she first discovered the Brontë sisters. Morgan lives in the Pacific Northwest of Canada with her husband, their three feral cats, one silly little dog, and ten thousand precarious piles of books and records. When she isn't dreaming up new and daring subplots or watching BBC documentaries while sipping tea and knitting a sweater, she is likely reading three books at once, playing Tetris, or planning her next *Buffy the Vampire Slayer* and/or *Doctor Who* marathon weekend. This is her first romance novel, though she publishes literary and speculative fiction as well. Morgan loves to hear from other readers and writers, so please feel free to visit her at www.morgankellyromance.com, where anyone can easily leave her their calling card after catching up on all the latest two-hundred-year-old gossip.

Give in to your impulses . . .
Read on for a sneak peek at two brand-new
e-book original tales of romance
from Avon Books.
Available now wherever e-books are sold.

THE FORBIDDEN LADY
By Kerrelyn Sparks

TURN TO DARKNESS
By Jaime Rush

An Excerpt from

THE FORBIDDEN LADY

by Kerrelyn Sparks

**(Originally published under
the title *For Love or Country*)**

Before *New York Times* bestselling author Kerrelyn Sparks
created a world of vampires, there was another world of spies
and romance . . .

Keep reading for a look at her very first novel.

Tuesday, August 29, 1769

"I say, dear gel, how much do *you* cost?"

Virginia's mouth dropped open. "I—I beg your pardon?"

The bewigged, bejeweled, and bedeviling man who faced her spoke again. "You're a fetching sight and quite sweet-smelling for a wench who has traveled for weeks, imprisoned on this godforsaken ship. I say, what *is* your price?"

She opened her mouth, but nothing came out. The rolling motion of the ship caught her off guard, and she stumbled, widening her stance to keep her balance. This man thought she was for sale? Even though they were on board *The North Star*, a brigantine newly arrived in Boston Harbor with a fresh supply of indentured servants, could he actually mistake her for one of the poor wretched criminals huddled near the front of the ship?

Her first reaction of shock was quickly replaced with anger. It swelled in her chest, heated to a quick boil, and soared past her ruffled neckline to her face, scorching her cheeks 'til she fully expected steam, instead of words, to escape her mouth.

"How . . . how *dare* you!" With gloved hands, she twisted the silken cords of her drawstring purse. "Pray, be gone with you, sir."

"Ah, a saucy one." The gentleman plucked a silver snuffbox from his lavender silk coat. He kept his tall frame erect to avoid flipping his wig, which was powdered with a lavender tint to match his coat. "Tsk, tsk, dear gel, such impertinence is sure to lower your price."

Her mouth fell open again.

Seizing the opportunity, he raised his quizzing glass and examined the conveniently opened orifice. "Hmm, but you do have excellent teeth."

She huffed. "And a sharp tongue to match."

"*Mon Dieu*, a very saucy mouth, indeed." He smiled, displaying straight, white teeth.

A perfectly bright smile, Virginia thought. What a pity his mental faculties were so dim in comparison. But she refrained from responding with an insulting remark. No good could come from stooping to his level of ill manners. She stepped back, intending to leave, but hesitated when he spoke again.

"I do so like your nose. Very becoming and—" He opened his silver box, removed a pinch of snuff with his gloved fingers and sniffed.

She waited for him to finish the sentence. He was a buffoon, to be sure, but she couldn't help but wonder—did he actually like her nose? Over the years, she had endured a great deal of teasing because of the way it turned up on the end.

He snapped his snuffbox shut with a click. "Ah, yes, where was I, becoming and . . . disdainfully haughty. Yes, that's it."

Heat pulsed to her face once more. "I daresay it is not surprising for *you* to admire something *disdainfully haughty*, but regardless of your opinion, it is improper for you to address me so rudely. For that matter, it is highly improper for you to speak to me at all, for need I remind you, sir, we have not been introduced."

He dropped his snuffbox back into his pocket. "Definitely disdainful. And haughty." His mouth curled up, revealing two dimples beneath the rouge on his cheeks.

She glared at the offensive fop. Somehow, she would give him the cut he deserved.

A short man in a brown buckram coat and breeches scurried toward them. "Mr. Stanton! The criminals for sale are over there, sir, near the forecastle. You see the ones in chains?"

Raising his quizzing glass, the lavender dandy pivoted on his high heels and perused the line of shackled prisoners. He shrugged his silk-clad shoulders and glanced back at Virginia with a look of feigned horror. "Oh, dear, what a delightful little *faux pas*. I suppose you're not for sale after all?"

"No, of course not."

"I do beg your pardon." He flipped a lacy, monogrammed handkerchief out of his chest pocket and made a poor attempt to conceal the wide grin on his face.

A heavy, flowery scent emanated from his handkerchief, nearly bowling her over. He was probably one of those people who never bathed, just poured on more perfume. She covered her mouth with a gloved hand and gently coughed.

"Well, no harm done." He waved his handkerchief in the

air. "*C'est la vie* and all that. Would you care for some snuff? 'Tis my own special blend from London, don't you know. We call it *Grey Mouton*."

"Gray sheep?"

"Why, yes. Sink me! You *parlez français*? How utterly charming for one of your class."

Narrowing her eyes, she considered strangling him with the drawstrings of her purse.

He removed the silver engraved box from his pocket and flicked it open. "A pinch, in the interest of peace?" His mouth twitched with amusement.

"No, thank you."

He lifted a pinch to his nose and sniffed. "What did I tell you, Johnson?" he asked the short man in brown buckram at his side. "These Colonials are a stubborn lot, far too eager to take offense"—he sneezed delicately into his lacy handkerchief—"and far too unappreciative of the efforts the mother country makes on their behalf." He slid his closed snuffbox back into his pocket.

Virginia planted her hands on her hips. "You speak, perhaps, of Britain's kindness in providing us with a steady stream of slaves?"

"Slaves?"

She gestured toward the raised platform of the forecastle, where Britain's latest human offering stood in front, chained at the ankles and waiting to be sold.

"Oh." He waved his scented handkerchief in dismissal. "You mean the indentured servants. They're not slaves, my dear, only criminals paying their dues to society. 'Tis the mother country's fervent hope they will be reformed by their experience in America."

"I see. Perhaps we should send the mother country a boatload of American wolves to see if they can be reformed by their experience in Britain?"

His chuckle was surprisingly deep. "*Touché.*"

The deep timbre of his voice reverberated through her skin, striking a chord that hummed from her chest down to her belly. She caught her breath and looked at him more closely. When his eyes met hers, his smile faded away. Time seemed to hold still for a moment as he held her gaze, quietly studying her.

The man in brown cleared his throat.

Virginia blinked and looked away. She breathed deeply to calm her racing heart. Once more, she became aware of the murmur of voices and the screech of sea gulls overhead. What had happened? It must have been the thrill of putting the man in his place that had affected her. Strange, though, that he had happily acknowledged her small victory.

Mr. Stanton gave the man in brown a mildly irritated look, then smiled at her once more. "American wolves, you say? Really, my dear, these people's crimes are too petty to compare them to murderous beasts. Why, Johnson, here, was an indentured servant before becoming my secretary. Were you not, Johnson?"

"Aye, Mr. Stanton," the older man answered. "But I came voluntarily. Not all these people are prisoners. The group to the right doesn't wear chains. They're selling themselves out of desperation."

"There, you see." The dandy spread his gloved hands, palms up, in a gesture of conciliation. "No hard feelings. In fact, I quite trust Johnson here with all my affairs in spite of his criminal background. You know the Colonials are quite wrong in thinking we British are a cold, callous lot."

Virginia gave Mr. Johnson a small, sympathetic smile, letting him know she understood his indenture had not been due to a criminal past. Her own father, faced with starvation and British cruelty, had left his beloved Scottish Highlands as an indentured servant. Her sympathy seemed unnecessary, however, for Mr. Johnson appeared unperturbed by his employer's rudeness. No doubt the poor man had grown accustomed to it.

She gave Mr. Stanton her stoniest of looks. "Thank you for enlightening me."

"My pleasure, dear gel. Now I must take my leave." Without further ado, he ambled toward the group of gaunt, shackled humans, his high-heeled shoes clunking on the ship's wooden deck and his short secretary tagging along behind.

Virginia scowled at his back. The British needed to go home, and the sooner, the better.

"I say, old man." She heard his voice filter back as he addressed his servant. "I do wish the pretty wench were for sale. A bit too saucy, perhaps, but I do so like a challenge. *Quel dommage*, a real pity, don't you know."

A vision of herself tackling the dandy and stuffing his lavender-tinted wig down his throat brought a smile to her lips. She could do it. Sometimes she pinned down her brother when he tormented her. Of course, such behavior might be frowned upon in Boston. This was not the hilly region of North Carolina that the Munro family called home.

And the dandy might prove difficult to knock down. Watching him from the back, she realized how large he was. She grimaced at the lavender bows on his high-heeled pumps. Why would a man that tall need to wear heels? Another pair of lavender bows served as garters, tied over the tabs of his silk knee breeches. His silken hose were too sheer to hide padding, so those calves were truly that muscular. *How odd.*

He didn't mince his steps like one would expect from a fopdoodle, but covered the deck with long, powerful strides, the walk of a man confident in his strength and masculinity.

She found herself examining every inch of him, calculating the amount of hard muscle hidden beneath the silken exterior. What color was his hair under that hideous tinted wig? Probably black, like his eyebrows. His eyes had gleamed like polished pewter, pale against his tanned face.

Her breath caught in her throat. A tanned face? A fop would not spend the necessary hours toiling in the sun that resulted in a bronzed complexion.

This Mr. Stanton was a puzzle.

She shook her head, determined to forget the perplexing man. Yet, if he dressed more like the men back home—tight buckskin breeches, boots, no wig, no lace . . .

The sun bore down with increasing heat, and she pulled her hand-painted fan from her purse and flicked it open. She breathed deeply as she fanned herself. Her face tingled with a mist of salty air and the lingering scent of Mr. Stanton's handkerchief.

She watched with growing suspicion as the man in question postured in front of the women prisoners with his quizzing glass, assessing them with a practiced eye. Oh, dear, what were the horrible man's intentions? She slipped her fan back into her purse and hastened to her father's side.

Jamie Munro was speaking quietly to a fettered youth who appeared a good five years younger than her one and twenty years. "All I ask, young man, is honesty and a good day's work. In exchange, ye'll have food, clean clothes, and a clean pallet."

The spindly boy's eyes lit up, and he licked his dry, chapped lips. "Food?"

Virginia's father nodded. "Aye. Mind you, ye willna be working for me, lad, but for my widowed sister, here, in Boston. Do ye have any experience as a servant?"

The boy lowered his head and shook it. He shuffled his feet, the scrape of his chains on the deck grating at Virginia's heart.

"Papa," she whispered.

Jamie held up a hand. "Doona fash yerself, lass. I'll be taking the boy."

As the boy looked up, his wide grin cracked the dried dirt on his cheeks. "Thank you, my lord."

Jamie winced. "Mr. Munro, it is. We'll have none of that lordy talk aboot here. Welcome to America." He extended a hand, which the boy timidly accepted. "What is yer name, lad?"

"George Peeper, sir."

"Father." Virginia tugged at the sleeve of his blue serge coat. "Can we afford any more?"

Jamie Munro's eyes widened and he blinked at his daughter. "More? Just an hour ago, ye upbraided me aboot the evils of purchasing people, and now ye want more? 'Tis no' like buying ribbons for yer bonny red hair."

"I know, but this is important." She leaned toward him. "Do you see the tall man in lavender silk?"

Jamie's nose wrinkled. "Aye. Who could miss him?"

"Well, he wanted to purchase me—"

"*What?*"

She pressed the palms of her hands against her father's broad chest as he moved to confront the dandy. "'Twas a misunderstanding. Please."

His blue eyes glittering with anger, Jamie clenched his fists. "Let me punch him for you, lass."

"No, listen to me. I fear he means to buy one of those ladies for . . . immoral purposes."

Jamie frowned at her. "And what would ye be knowing of a man's immoral purposes?"

"Father, I grew up on a farm. I can make certain deductions, and I know from the way he looked at me, the man is not looking for someone to scrub his pots."

"What can I do aboot it?"

"If he decides he wants one, you could outbid him."

"He would just buy another, Ginny. I canna be buying the whole ship. I can scarcely afford this one here."

She bit her lip, considering. "You could buy one more if Aunt Mary pays for George. She can afford it much more than we."

"Nay." Jamie shook his head. "I willna have my sister paying. This is the least I can do to help Mary before we leave.

Besides, I seriously doubt I could outbid the dandy even once. Look at the rich way he's dressed, though I havena stet clue why a man would spend good coin to look like that."

The ship rocked suddenly, and Virginia held fast to her father's arm. A breeze wafted past her, carrying the scent of unwashed bodies. She wrinkled her nose. She should have displayed the foresight to bring a scented handkerchief, though not as overpowering as the one sported by the lavender popinjay.

Having completed his leisurely perusal of the women, Mr. Stanton was now conversing quietly with a young boy.

"Look, Father, that boy is so young to be all alone. He cannot be more than ten."

"Aye," Jamie replied. "We can only hope a good family will be taking him in."

"How much for the boy?" Mr. Stanton demanded in a loud voice.

The captain answered, "You'll be thinking twice before taking that one. He's an expensive little wretch."

Mr. Stanton lowered his voice. "Why is that?"

"I'll be needing payment for his passage *and* his mother's. The silly tart died on the voyage, so the boy owes you fourteen years of labor."

The boy swung around and shook a fist at the captain. "Me mum was not a tart, ye bloody old bugger!"

The captain yelled back, "And he has a foul mouth, as you can see. You'll be taking the strap to him before the day is out."

Virginia squeezed her father's arm. "The boy is responsible for his mother's debt?"

"Aye." Jamie nodded. "'Tis how it works."

Mr. Stanton adjusted the lace on his sleeves. "I have a fancy to be extravagant today. Name your price."

"At least the poor boy will have a roof over his head and food to eat." Virginia grimaced. "I only hope the dandy will not dress him in lavender silk."

Jamie Munro frowned. "Oh, dear."

"What is it, Father?"

"Ye say the man was interested in you, Ginny?"

"Aye, he seemed to like me in his own horrid way."

"Hmm. Perhaps the lad will be all right. At any rate, 'tis too late now. Let me pay for George, and we'll be on our way."

An Excerpt from

TURN TO DARKNESS

by Jaime Rush

Enter the world of the Offspring with this latest novella in Jaime Rush's fabulous paranormal series.

CHAPTER ONE

When Shea Baker pulled into her driveway, the sight of Darius's black coupe in front of her little rented house annoyed her. That it wasn't Greer's Jeep, and that she was disappointed it wasn't, annoyed the hell out of her.

Darius pulled out his partially dismantled wheelchair from inside the car and put it together within a few seconds. His slide from the driver's seat into his wheelchair was so practiced it was almost fluid. He waved, oblivious to her frown, and wheeled over to her truck. "As pale as you looked after hearing what Tucker, Del, and I went through, I thought you'd go right home." He wore his dark blond hair in a James Dean style, his waves gelled to stand up.

She *had* been freaked. Two men trying to kill them, men who would kill them all if they knew about their existence. She yanked her baseball cap lower on her head, a nervous habit. "I had a couple of jobs to check on. What brings you by?" She hoped it was something quick he could tell her right there and leave.

"Tucker kicked me out. I think he feels threatened by me,

because I had to take charge. I saved the day, and he won't even admit it."

None of the guys were comfortable with Darius. His mercurial mood shifts and oversized ego were irritating, but the shadows in his eyes hinted at an affinity for violence. In the two years he'd lived with them, though, he'd mostly kept to himself. She'd had no problem with him because he remained aloof, never revealing his emotions, even when he talked about the car accident that had taken his mobility. Unfortunately, when he thought she was reaching out to him, that aloofness had changed to romantic interest.

"Sounded like you went off the rails." She crossed her arms in front of her. "Look, if you're here to get me on your side, I won't—"

"I'd never ask you to do that." His upper lip lifted in a sneer. "I know you're loyal only to Tucker."

She narrowed her eyes, her body stiffening. "Tuck's like a big brother to me. He gave me a home when I was on the streets, told me why I have extraordinary powers." That she'd inherited DNA from another dimension was crazy-wild, but it made as much sense as, say, being able to move objects with her mind. "I'd take his side over anyone's."

"Wish someone would feel that kind of loyalty to me," Darius muttered under his breath, making her wonder if he was trying to elicit her sympathy. "I get that you're brotherly/sisterly." He let those words settle for a second. "But something happened with you and Greer, didn't it? What did he do, grope you?"

"Don't be ridiculous. Greer would never do something like that."

"Something happened, because all of a sudden the way you looked at each other changed. Like he was way interested in you, and you were way uncomfortable around him. Then you sat all close to me, and I know you felt the same electricity I did."

She shook her head, sending her curly ponytail swinging over her shoulder. "There was no electricity. Greer and I had a . . . disagreement. I needed to put some space between us, but when you live in a house with four other people, there isn't a lot of room. When I sat next to you, I was just moving away from him."

Darius's shoulders, wide and muscular, stiffened. "You might think that, Shea. You might even believe it. But someday you're going to realize you want me. And when you do, I want you to know I can satisfy you. When I'm in Darkness, I'm a whole man." That dark glint in his eyes hinted at his arrogance. "I'm capable of anything."

Those words shivered through her, but not in the way he'd intended. In that moment, she knew somehow that he *was* capable of anything. Darius might be confined to a wheelchair, but only a fool would underestimate him, and she was no fool. Especially where Darkness was concerned. The guys possessed it, yet didn't know exactly what it was. All they knew was that they'd probably inherited it, along with the DNA that gave them extraordinary powers, from the men who'd gotten their mothers pregnant. It allowed them to Become something far from human.

"Please, Darius, don't talk to me about that kind of thing. I'm not interested in having sex with anyone."

The corner of his mouth twisted cruelly. "Don't you like

sex? Maybe you've never been with someone who could do it well."

For a long time the thought of sex had coated her in shame and disgust. Until that little incident with Greer, when she'd had a totally different—and surprising—reaction.

"Look, I'm sorry Tuck kicked you out, but I don't have a guest bedroom."

"I'll sleep on the couch. You won't even know I'm here." His face transformed from darkly sexual to a happy little boy's. "I don't have any other place to stay," he added, building his case. "You just said how grateful you are to Tuck for taking you in. I'm only asking for the same thing."

Damn, he had her. As much as she wanted to squash her feelings, some things did reach right under her shields. And some people . . . like Greer. Now, Darius's manipulation did. "All right," she spat out, feeling pinned.

Her phone rang from where she'd left it inside her truck.

"Thanks, Shea," Darius said, wheeling to his car and popping the trunk. "You're a doll."

She got into her truck, grabbing up the phone and eyeing the screen. Greer. She'd been trying to avoid him since moving out three months before. But with the weirdness going on lately, she needed to stay in the loop.

"Hey," she answered. "What's up?"

"Tuck and Darius had it out a while ago. Darius has this idea about being the alpha male, which is just stupid, and Tuck kicked him out. I wanted to let you know in case he shows up on your doorstep pulling his 'poor me' act."

"Too late," she said in a singsong voice. "Act pulled—very well, I might add. He's staying for a few days."

"Bad idea." Always the protective one. He made no apologies for it either.

She watched Darius lift his suitcase onto his lap and wheel toward the ramp he'd installed for wheelchair access to her front door. "Well, what was I supposed to do, turn him away? I don't like it either."

"I'm coming over."

"There's no need . . ." She looked at the screen, blinking to indicate he'd ended the call. ". . . to come over," she finished anyway.

She got out, feeling like her feet weighed fifty pounds each, and trudged to the door. All she wanted was to be alone, a quiet evening trimming her bonsai to clear her mind.

There would be no mind-clearing tonight. There'd be friction between Greer and Darius, just like there had been before she'd moved out. Tuck had eased her into the reality of Darkness, he and Greer morphing into black beasts only after she'd accepted the idea. Tuck told her it also made them fiercely, and insanely, territorial about their so-called mates. She hadn't thought twice about that until Darius and Greer both took a different kind of liking to her. She was afraid they'd tear each other's throats out, and she wasn't either of their mates.

"Two days," she said, unlocking her front door. "I like living on my own. Being alone." Most of the time. It was strange, but she'd sit at her table in the mornings having coffee (not as strong as Greer's k iller brew) and be happy about being alone. Then she'd get hit with a wave of sadness about being alone.

See how messed up you are.

"You might like having me around," he said. "If that guy

who's been creeping around makes an appearance, I'll kick his ass."

"Well, he's too much of a coward to knock on the door." She didn't want to think about her stalker. He hadn't left any of his icky letters or "gifts" in a few days.

She figured out where Darius could stash his suitcases and was hunting down extra sheets and a blanket when the doorbell rang. Before she could even set the extra pillow down to answer, she heard Darius's voice: "Well, look who's here. What a nice surprise."

Not by the tone in his voice. Damn, this was so not cool having them both here. They'd been like snarling dogs the day everyone had helped her move in here. She hadn't had them over since.

She walked out holding the pillow to her chest like a shield. Greer's eyes went right to her, giving her a clear *Is everything all right?* look.

She wasn't in danger. That's as far as she'd commit.

Greer closed the door and sauntered in, as though he always stopped by. "Thought I'd check in on you. After what happened, figured you might be on edge." There he went again, sinking her into the depths of his eyes. They were rimmed in gray, brown in the middle, the most unusual eyes she'd ever seen. And they were assessing her.

"She's fine," Darius answered as she opened her mouth. "I'm staying here for a couple of days, which will work out nicely . . . in case she's on edge." His unspoken *So you can go now* was clear.

Greer moved closer to her, putting himself physically between her and Darius. He was a damned wall of a man, too, way tall, wide shoulders, and just big. He purposely blocked Darius's view of her.

She'd done this, sparked them into hostile territory. Which was laughable, considering what she looked like: baggy pants and shirt, cap over her head, no makeup. She'd done everything she could for the last six years to squash every bit of her femininity. Her sexuality. Then Greer had blown that to bits.

He hadn't knocked, just barged into the bathroom, a towel loosely held in front of his naked body. She was drying her hair and suddenly he was standing there gaping at her.

"Jesus, Shea, you're beautiful," he'd said, obviously in shock.

She couldn't move, spellbound herself, which was ridiculous because she wasn't interested in anyone sexually. But there stood six feet four of olive-skinned Apache with muscled thighs and a scant bit of towel covering him. And the way he'd said those words, with his typical passion, and his looking at her like she *was* beautiful and he wanted her, woke up something inside her.

Breaking out of the spell and wrapping her towel around her, she'd yelled at him for barging in, stepping up close to him and jabbing her finger at his chest.

And what had he done? Lifted her damp hair from her shoulders, hair she never left loose, his fingers brushing her bare shoulders. "Why do you hide yourself from us?" he'd asked.

"Don't say anything about this to anyone." Would he tell them how oversized her breasts were? Would they wonder why she hid her curves, talking behind her back, speculating? "Leave. Now."

He'd shrugged, his dark brown eyebrows furrowing. "No

need to get mad or freaked out. It was an accident. We're friends."

He left, finally, and she looked in the steamy reflection. She didn't see beautiful. But she did see hunger, and even worse, felt it.

"How's your big job coming?" Greer asked now, pulling her out of the memory. He was leaning against the back of the couch, which inadvertently flexed the muscles in his arms.

He remembered, which touched her even if she didn't want to be touched. Still, she found herself smiling. "Great. We're putting the finishing touches now that the hard-scaping and most of the planting is finished. This is my biggest job yet. My business has kept me sane through all this. Gotta keep working on the customer's jobs." She glanced to the window. If the sun weren't going to be setting soon, she'd come up with some job she had to zip off to right then.

Dammit, she missed Greer. Hated having to shut him out. Now, things were odd between them. He looked at her differently, heat in his eyes, and hurt, too, because he didn't understand why she'd pushed him away. Like he'd said, it was an accident that he'd walked in on her.

"Do you want to stay for dinner?" she asked, not sure whether having them both there would be better than being alone with Darius.

Greer glanced at his watch. "Wish I could. My shift starts in an hour."

Darius wheeled up. "Yeah, the big bad firefighter, off to save lives." He made a superhero arm motion, pumping one fist in the air.

Greer's mouth twisted in a snarl. "I'd rather do that than tinker with computer parts all day."

"Boys," she said, sounding like a teacher.

Another knock on the door. Hopefully it was Tucker. He was good at stepping in. But it wasn't Tucker. Two men stood there, their badges at the ready. "Cheyenne Baker?" one of them asked.

She nodded, feeling Greer step up behind her.

"Detective Dan Marshall, and Detective Paul Marron. May we come in?"

"What's this about?" Greer asked before she could say anything.

"We have some questions about a recent incident." The man, in his forties, waited patiently for someone to invite them inside.

Greer inspected the badge, nodded to her. It was legit.

Shea checked it, too, then stepped back, bumping into Greer. "These are friends of mine," she said, waving to Greer and Darius.

Marshall closed the door behind them, taking in both men as though noting their appearance. He focused on her. "You've heard about the man who was mauled two nights ago?"

Her mouth went dry. How had they connected that to her? Bad enough that it triggered two men from the other dimension to hunt down their offspring. "Yes, it sounded horrible." She shuddered, and didn't have to fake it. "Wild animals attacking people in their own home."

"We don't think it was a wild animal. Do you know Fred Callahan, the victim?"

"No, I—" Her words jammed in her throat when she saw the picture he held up, a driver's license photo probably. All the blood drained from her face. "I knew him as Frankie C." She cleared the fuzz from her voice. "I haven't seen him for six years." She wanted the cops to go, or for Greer and Darius to leave. "I'm sorry, I can't help you."

Marshall's eyes flicked to Greer and Darius before returning to her. "We found pictures and notes about you on his computer. There was a letter in his desk drawer addressed to you, indicating he'd written to you before. It wasn't a very nice letter."

Her knees went weak. Greer somehow sensed it and clamped his hands on her shoulders. "What are you insinuating?" His hands started warming her, one of his psychic abilities.

Darius wheeled closer. "You can't possibly think this slip of a girl could tear a man apart."

"I've been getting letters, creepy gifts," she said. "But I didn't know who they were from." Frankie. She had wondered, yes, but how had he found her? And why after all these years?

"May I see them?" Marshall asked.

She'd wanted to throw them away, but thought they might be evidence if things escalated. She went to the file cabinet in her office and returned with the letters, and the box.

Marshall frowned when he opened it and saw the dildo, the flavored lube creams. "Can I take these?"

"Please." *And go. Say no more.*

He looked at Greer and Darius. "Did either of you know who was harassing her?"

Darius snorted. "No, but I'm glad the sick fu—the guy is dead. It's wrong to harass a woman like that."

Greer shook his head, but his gaze was on her.

Marshall turned to her again. "Callahan worked at the phone company. That's probably how he found you. You haven't heard from him at all in the six years since you filed charges against him and the other two men?"

"No, nothing," she said quickly. "I'd rather not—"

"I'm sure the detective you spoke to talked you out of going forward with the charges. I read the file and agree that it was a long shot to prosecute the case successfully. Still, I wish we had. One of those other men raped a teenaged girl a couple of years back. He's in prison now. The other's been jailed a few times on battery charges."

She felt Greer's questioning stare on her. "I'm sorry to hear that." Her words sounded shaky. *Leave, dammit.*

Marshall glanced in the box, then her. "But Callahan hasn't had another brush with the law. We did find some rather disturbing items in his home, including sex toys I presume he intended to send to you. One was a pair of handcuffs, and they weren't the fuzzy kind. It's the sort of thing that makes me uncomfortable about where he was going with this. So if you"—he looked at her friends—"or anyone had something to do with his death, it may have saved your life. But still, we have to investigate. It's a crime to tear a man apart, no matter how much of a scumbag he is."

"Son of a bitch," Greer said. His hands tightened on her as she slumped against the couch, and then he pulled her against his body, his arms like a shield over her collarbone.

Oh, God. Had Frankie been planning to rape her again? That overshadowed anything else in her mind at the moment.

Marshall seemed to be giving them time to fess up.

"We didn't know who the guy sending that stuff was," Shea said. "You can see from the letters that he never signed them." They'd been crude letters, detailing what he wanted to do to her body, and she'd forced herself to read them because she needed to know how much he knew about her. Or if they contained an explicit threat.

"Was it because of your earlier experience that you didn't report the stalking?" Marshall asked.

She shrugged, though it felt as though she wore an armored suit that smelled of a citrus cologne. "I didn't see it as threatening. Only gross and annoying."

Wrapped in Greer's embrace, she felt safe in a sea of chaos.

Marshall gave her his business card. "If there's anything else you know or remember, please give me a call." He took a step toward the door but turned back to her. "Ms. Baker, if anyone ever hurts you like that again, call me."

As soon as he left, Darius wheeled in front of her. "The guy's dead, Shea. You don't have to worry about him anymore. Isn't that great?"

Thank God Darius hadn't asked for more information. If only Greer would let it go.

He turned her to face him. "What happened? What was he talking about, if you're hurt 'again'?" His concern turned her to mush, and then his expression changed. He cradled her face, and as much as she wanted to push away, she couldn't. "Oh, Shea."

She heard it all in his voice—that he'd figured it out from

the detective's words. Raped "another" woman. She felt her expression crumple even though she tried to hold strong.

He pulled her against him, stroking her back. Her cap's brim bumped against him and it fell to the floor.

No, she had to push away. She would fall apart right here, and he would continue to hold her and soothe her, and it felt so good because no one had done that afterward. Not even her mother, who had the same opinion the cops did: that she deserved it.

She managed to move out of his embrace by reaching for her cap. She shoved it onto her head, pulling down the brim. "I'm fine. It was a long time ago."

"What are you two talking about?" Darius asked. At least he hadn't gotten it.

That was the difference between them, one of many. She wondered if Darius just had no emotions, nothing to squash or tuck away.

"You'd better go," she said to Greer, her voice thick. "You don't want to be late for your shift."

He was looking at her, probably giving her the same look he'd been giving her since the bathroom incident. The *Why are you shutting me out?* one. She couldn't tell, thankfully, because the brim of her cap blocked his eyes from view. At least he'd also pushed back after the bathroom incident and gone on, continued dating. He'd been cool to her afterward. That's what she wanted. Even if it stuck a knife in her chest.

"I do have to go. Walk me out." He took her hand, giving her no choice but to be dragged along with him.

The air was even more chilling now that the sun was setting. He paused by his Jeep, turning her to face him. "Shea, that's why you hide yourself, isn't it? Why you freaked when I accidentally saw you naked." He pulled off her cap. "Three of them?" His agony at the thought wracked his face.

"I don't want to discuss this. I freaked because I don't want people to see me naked."

"Because you've got curves—"

She pressed her hand over his mouth, feeling the full softness of it. "I am not interested in discussing my curves or my past."

"You're hurting, Shea. It's why you shut down on me. I lost a friend once, because he was hurting, too. Holding in a painful secret. I left for a while, doing construction out of town, and when I came back, he'd taken his life. He couldn't take the pain anymore."

"I'm not going to take my life. I've survived, gotten over it—"

"You haven't gotten over it." He tugged at her oversized shirt. "You hide your body. All those years you lived with us, you hid yourself. Did you think we'd hurt you? Attack you?"

He had no idea. "Of course not."

"That's why you were so pissed about me seeing you. Your secret was out."

That he had right. "That's ridiculous." She took the opportunity to look down at her attire, to escape those assessing eyes. "This is just how I like to dress."

He took his finger and lifted her chin. "I suddenly saw you as a woman and not just the girl who's lived with us for the past few years. Seeing you as a woman changed everything."

She smacked his arm, which probably hurt her more than him. "Then change it back. I don't want you like that."

He slowly blinked at her statement. "Is it because of what happened to you? We can work through that."

"Is he bothering you?" Darius called from the front step.

Greer muttered something very impolite under his breath, and then said, louder, "Go back in the house. We're talking."

Darius started to wheel down the ramp. "Whatever concerns Shea concerns me, too."

"I'm going in now," she said, dashing off before Darius could get close. As she suspected, he turned around and followed her back to the front step. Greer stayed by his vehicle, giving Darius a pissed look. She was glad Darius had stopped that conversation. Way too close for comfort on many levels.

"I'm fine, Greer," she called to him. "Thanks for caring. Get to work."

"Did I interrupt a tense moment?" Darius asked once he'd caught up to her, watching Greer's yellow Jeep back out. "Looked like he was harassing you. It had to do with whatever he did to you, didn't it? Tell me, and I'll make sure—"

"It's none of your business." She stalked into the house to find something for dinner, anything to get her mind off what just transpired.

It was hard to think about spaghetti or leftover steak when one question dominated her mind: how could it be a coincidence that the man who had been mauled was her rapist?